Just A Little Later
With Eevo and Sim

Henry Shykoff

**Illustrated by
Marilyn Mets & Peter Ledwon**

To Joshua and Natalie

Henry Shykoff

Just a Little Later With Eevo and Sim
Henry Shykoff

Published by Natural Heritage/Natural History Inc.
P.O. Box 95, Station O, Toronto, Ontario M4A 2M8

National Library of Canada Cataloguing in Publication Data

Shykoff, Henry
    . Just a little later with Eevo and Sim

Continuation of: Once upon a time long, long ago.
ISBN 1-896219-73-X

        1. Prehistoric peoples—Juvenile fiction. I. Mets, Marilyn
II. Ledwon, Peter III. Shykoff, Henry. Once upon a time long, long ago. IV. Title.

PS8587.H94J88 2001   jC813'.54 C2001-902802-4
PZ7.S56266Ju 2001

Cover, illustrations and text design by Marilyn Mets & Peter Ledwon
Edited by Jane Gibson
Printed and bound in Canada by Hignell Printing Limited, Winnipeg, Manitoba.

The Canada Council | Le Conseil des Arts
for the Arts | du Canada

ONTARIO ARTS COUNCIL
CONSEIL DES ARTS DE L'ONTARIO

Natural Heritage / Natural History Inc. acknowledges the financial support of the Canada Council for the Arts and the Ontario Arts Council for our publishing program. We also acknowledge the financial support of the Government of Canada through the Book Publishing Industry Development Program (BPIDP) and the Association for the Export of Canadian Books.

Table of Contents

Prologue

This is the continuation of *Once Upon a Time, Long, Long Ago*, the adventures of Eevo and Sim. The story is set about 50,000 years ago, in the time of prehistoric man. Their parents, Shim and Dedu, have just returned from their long trip to the Wetlands Clan, the former home of Shim, their mother. They had gone to replace the much-needed flint knife, which originally had been made by Seer, Shim's father. While they were away from their home in the Cave Clan, their son, Sim, then about ten years old, had been driven out of the cave and left to die in the wilderness. The clan people considered him useless since he was lame and not able to help with hunting for food. Their food supply for the coming cold season was dangerously low. His twelve-year-old sister, Eevo, runs from the safety of the clan to help her brother. Together, Eevo and Sim overcame many dangers, discovered fire, rescued a pair of wolf cubs and saved the clan from starvation, and later from a sabre-tooth tiger.

When Dedu and Shim return with a supply of flint tools, they discover that Sim and Eevo have succeeded in making their own flint weapons. Upset by the discovery of what their Cave Clan had done to the two young people, they decide to return to Seer at the Wetlands Clan. Preparations have been made and they are about to set off on a long, dangerous journey, with more adventures for Eevo and Sim.

List of Characters

CAVE CLAN

Eevo: Young girl, about thirteen years old; the Fire Maker.

Sim: Her very curious brother, about eleven years old; a young flint knapper. Sim has a club foot.

Shim: Their mother, a very able woman; the first "outsider" member of the Cave Clan.

Dedu: Shim's mate and the best hunter of the Cave Clan.

Ab: Dedu's best friend, also a good hunter; possibly a half-brother.

Ree and Ur: Two young women in their teens; friends of Eevo and Sim; Keepers of the Fire for the Cave Clan; Ree is now Ab's mate.

Og: A skilled young hunter; he is now Ur's mate.

Old Hunter: The oldest member of the Cave Clan; the patriarch.

Neeth and Grosh: The female wolves raised by Eevo and Sim.

WETLANDS CLAN

Seer: Shim's father; he is the old flint knapper; the elder and leader of the clan.

Mee: A four-year-old girl.

Kno: Mee's mother.

OTHERS

Ola: A young man from the very distant Great River Clan.

Grew: The leader of the Salt Water Clan.

Sill: The leader of the Good Water Clan.

Loo: Sill's mate.

Lar: The Chief Fire Warden of the Great River Clan.

One

The Journey

They were going. Finally! Eevo and Sim could hardly wait. New people to meet, new places to explore. The plan had been to leave early, just after sunrise, but the tearful farewells had taken longer. They would miss their friends Ur and Ree, now the "Keepers of the Fire," and Og and Ab. Even Old Hunter had come to see them off. Already it was mid-morning, but now, there would be no more delays, only the long trek ahead. They could have started a full moon sooner, but Dedu had insisted that everything be just so. That included the weather. He wanted cool weather for walking across the sands. He also wanted plenty of water and to know that the water bags were tested for leakage before starting. Would the smoked meat that Shim had prepared for carrying be enough? Sim found it strange that his father was so fussy about things that seemed of so little consequence. But Dedu said that with good planning, a hard trip could be easy.

He was right. It was a wonderful trip. As the four of them, Shim, Dedu, Eevo and Sim, along with the two wolves headed off to the Wetlands clan, their mother's former home, the land changed from open grassland to hill country. There were fast flowing rivulets, plunging down like rapids, and waterfalls that became slow pleasant streams following the valley-bottom lands. The trees were adorned with fall colours and birds could be heard. At night they slept beside their fire, under the stars, wrapped snugly in their sleeping furs. Now, four days after their start, they could see a huge mountain ahead of them.

"How do we get over that?" asked Sim.

"We don't," replied Dedu.

"Then how ...?" began Sim.

"We keep to our left and swing around it," interjected Mother. "And right there, that's where the sands begin. Then you'll see why we were so careful about our water. The sand seems to stretch forever — and no water. Our first crossing was dreadful! This time we're ready."

It was the last night before the desert. The wolves had gone for their nightly prowl and the others prepared to sleep. The next day would test their ability to survive.

"Dedu, do you think you'll find that cool cave we used?" Shim asked anxiously.

Dedu, intent on watching a goat high above them, thinking about the food it could provide, grunted "Yes."

Eevo and Sim were trying to imagine what lay ahead.

"Tomorrow we leave this high country and go down to the sands," said Shim. "It will become very warm. But there is a spring of fresh water and a pool. We'll cool off and fill our water bags. From there it's about a quarter day's walk to that cave near the beginning of the sand country. We'll try to sleep there for the rest of the day. In the cool of the evening, we'll start across the sands."

Eevo and Sim were surprised, even though Shim had tried to prepare them. It was very hot in the lowlands. The pool was good but unexpectedly cold. Dedu just wet one foot. Even the wolves were hesitant — usually they enjoyed a splash in water.

This was the beginning of their first unpleasant day. Even the cave was not as expected. It too was hot, not cool at all. Late in the afternoon they awoke, covered in sweat. Something was very wrong. What was happening? Cautiously, they crept to the opening of the cave. Both wolves, however, did not budge. They lay very still, their heads resting on their paws, but with eyes wide open.

Two

Sandstorm

There was no sky. There was only sand, with sand-coloured light and a complete absence of shadows. No sky, no horizon, no sun! Only wind, wind-borne sand, and unbelievable heat! Sand was everywhere. Even at the entrance of the cave it clung to their sweaty skin. It was in their mouths. Their teeth felt gritty. Nothing was free of sand. The brisk wind veered about, blowing sand that seemed to come from all directions at once. The heat was overpowering. Just to stand upright was exhausting. It was far too hot to try to cross the sand lands, even this late in the day. Besides, it was impossible to see.

They waited in the shelter of the cave. Shim redid the harness she had made for the water bags, making the straps a little wider so that they would not dig so deeply into Dedu's shoulders. Water was much heavier than they had anticipated. Sim's suggestion that they carry a smaller amount was not accepted. Dedu wanted those water bags full. Experience had taught him not to venture into the desert without sufficient water. Had the stream and pool not been so far back, they would have returned there to cool off.

By evening, the wind has lessened but continued to blow from the direction in which they planned to go, heading directly towards them. But, visibility was improving and things seemed much better. The four humans, accompanied by their loyal wolves, set out for the two-day crossing of the sands.

That night the lights in the sky could not be seen. It was very dark. Much of the time, it was only the steady wind in their faces that told them which way they were going. They plodded on. Eventually there was just a hint of light in the sky, and it felt as if it should be about dawn. To their left there seemed to be a suggestion of a huge mass of land rising up towards the sky, in the direction where the mountain should be. Dedu felt relieved. He now knew where they were —a little more than halfway across the sands. But the sun was still not seen. All around, the sky was a reddish colour and the powerful wind shifted to blowing from their right. The sand it carried stung wherever it hit exposed skin. Eevo pulled her rabbit sleeping-fur from the pack on her back to make a face covering. The others did the same, soon however, it was almost impossible to breathe.

The noise of the wind became a wailing scream, making talk impossible. No one, not even Dedu, knew where they were. Nor could they tell in what direction they should travel. Soon that did not matter. There was only one direction they could move — with the wind. The wolves took the lead, and the group, with shoulders hunched, moved slowly forward. By now it was almost impossible to see. Moving closer to Grosh, Sim reached forward to grasp her tail. He groped about for Eevo and felt her beside him. He reached for her hand, and felt Neeth's nose almost touching Eevo. Close behind, Dedu and Mother walked hand-in-hand, with Dedu's free hand holding the shaft of the spear strapped to Sim's pack.

As the strongest person, Dedu carried the large water bag harnessed over his shoulder. Shim hauled all of the food, except for the emergency portions that each carried in neck pouches. Eevo, being more sure-footed than Sim, had the smaller water bag. Underfoot were millions and millions of very fine particles of sand. Sometimes the surface was hard-packed, but at other times their feet sank in beyond the ankle. Every step was hard work.

Struggling up a very steep sand dune, Mother hit a loose section and lost her footing. Dedu tried to stop her slide, but was pulled down with her. As he fell, he lost his hold on the shaft of the spear. Sim did not know.

Mother's ankle twisted as she hit the bottom of the dune. She cried out in pain, but no one could hear her over the howl of the wind. Dedu helped her up, but Shim could not stand. He shouted to Sim and Eevo, but his words were blown back to him. In just that short time, the others disappeared from view and continued on, unaware that they were now separated from their parents.

Shim and Dedu found that the steep dune they had slipped down was created by the sand piling up against a rocky outcrop. The area behind was in the lee of the wind, creating just what Dedu needed — a little sheltered area. He helped Shim wiggle into this little space, and they took cover behind this rocky reef. Once out of the direct wind, things improved. The sand no longer bit their skin, but the sound of the wind was deafening.

Digging down into the sand, Dedu scooped with his hands to enlarge their shelter. The wind, whipping around the rocky obstruction, added sand to both sides of the nest they had made for themselves. There was, however, some danger in this. If the sides became too high, they might collapse and bury them. When the side grew about as high as Dedu, he loosened the sand on top with the butt of his spear and the wind blew away the disturbed sand. They had to do this again and again. There was nothing they could do but wait out the storm. This gave them both plenty of time to worry about Sim, Eevo and the wolves, and to wonder why they had even suggested such a journey. The great roar of the wind made it impossible to talk, so each was alone with her and his thoughts.

Shim's mind flashed back to their planning. By waiting as they did, they had thought their crossing of the sand would be at a cooler, safer time. Every possibility had been considered. Nothing could go wrong, and now this. Eevo and Sim had never been in the desert. They were going further and further into unknown territory. What would happen to them? Shim knew they were capable; their survival on their own had proven that. But being lost in a fierce desert sandstorm is something few hunters survive. They were only children. Why had they left the safety of their clan anyway?

But they had water. No one before them had. They had water because Dedu had asked, "How can we carry water?" Everyone had tried making containers out of cured skins, covering the stitch holes with the gum that came from some of the softwood trees. But everything leaked. It was a remark made in jest that gave Sim an idea. Og had remarked with a chuckle that rabbit stomachs might do, but they were too little. Sim, remembering the size of the stomach of the great elk they had killed, exclaimed, "That's it! What about an elk stomach? One of those could carry enough water for a few days." With the help of the wolves, Sim, Dedu, Ab and Og had killed an elk. They opened its belly and Sim fed most of the entrails to the wolves, but the stomach and bladder were removed with care.

Shim took over the job of making the water bags. She turned the stomach inside out and scraped off the inner lining. Then she smoked the whole stomach over a small fire for the rest of the day, keeping it well away from the fire for fear of burning it. Once they tied off the bottom bit of intestine, they had a watertight bag. When they filled it with water, it held without leaking. Once the narrow upper opening was tied with a piece of gut, the stomach bag could be carried in any position with no spillage of water. While the water did have a smoky taste, it was not bad for drinking. The same thing was done with the bladder. Now they had two water containers, one large and one smaller.

The elk meat that Dedu has brought back had been cut into thin slices, smoked over a slow fire and put out to dry in the sunlight. This was their supply of meat for the trip. Because of this food, she and Dedu were not in serious danger —not as yet anyway. The storm had to stop sometime. No, they were not in danger, but Eevo and Sim had only the small water bag and a little food. Did they know the route? Had either she or Dedu told them about the landmarks to use? If her memory was correct, she had told him. Sim would remember. She relaxed a little.

Dedu, however, sat still, fingering the new club that Sim had designed and made for him. Old Hunter had said that he was too weak now to use a tree branch club. This had given Sim the idea for a new kind of club. Dedu remembered him going to his woodpile and looking through it until he found a shaft of wood about as long as his leg and thigh.

Dedu remembered saying, "Don't you think that is too short to make a useful spear? The thickness of the shaft is one that would suit my hand. The whole thing is no longer than a club, but it is far too thin!"

Sim had answered by talking about a new weapon for Old Hunter, one that did not require Dedu's strength. He then picked up an oval piece of flint a little longer and wider than his outstretched hand, and about twice its thickness. With a few careful taps from a hammer stone, he had flaked the two ends into ragged but sharp cutting edges. This large piece of flint was set into the notch in the shaft and tied in place with many wrappings of wet rawhide cord, so that the flint was held firmly. Since the rawhide shrank when it dried, the flint head and the wooden shaft would be as if they were one. He now had a lightweight flint club that could be used by almost anyone, unlike the heavy awkward tree branches they had been using. Despite its light weight, it was a far more effective hunting weapon. Sim had passed the axe to Dedu. He remembered swinging it and examining the attachment of flint to wood. He had called Ab over. Both were very impressed.

14

This special club had been given to him, and Sim had made one for Ab and a lighter one for Old Hunter. In so many ways both Sim and Eevo had shown just how capable they were at hunting.

Shim thought about the wolves. She remembered a large grey head was resting on her lap and being stroked. She had begun to talk to the wolf.

"You are a wonderful friend," she murmured, "and you should have a name. I will call you Neeth. That means 'a wonderful friend' in my clan's language. I will call your sister Grosh, which means 'watchful'. "

The wolf lay completely relaxed, almost asleep. Its soft breathing in turn lulled her so that she too fell asleep. She remembered waking when Dedu made some noise on coming out of the cave. He found her with her head lying on the wolf's flank and her right arm flung over its body. The wolf's head, with one eye open watching him, was resting on her lap. Laughing, she had told Dedu and then the others that she had given each wolf a name. They all liked her choices. From that time on, the wolves were spoken to and called by name. Before long, they recognized and responded to their names.

Everything they could have done had been done. It should be an easy trip to the Wetlands Clan. Once the final farewells were said, they had left. The morning had dawned, a bright day, one with a crisp feel to the air and with leaves falling from the trees and littering the ground every time there was a gust of cold wind. They started toward the hills where Eevo and Sim had seen the fire that night they had planned to look for them, their parents. Five moons had passed and now they and their children were separated again. Eevo and Sim were on their own in a sandstorm. Their survival depended on their own ability, and on luck. She and Dedu could do no more than keep themselves alive and hope.

Sim became aware that Dedu was no longer holding on to the spear shaft when he turned suddenly as Grosh changed direction. The spear shaft moved freely. There was no resistance to its swing. He managed to stop both Grosh and Neeth. "They're not behind us!" he shouted into Eevo's ear. He turned and tried to look through the fog of sand particles. It was useless. Eevo tried too, with similar results.

"Do you know when we lost them?" she shouted in return.

"No," he answered. "We'll have to turn back."

"No," Eevo shouted. "No! We don't know where back is. And we can't stay here. Let's follow the wolves and try to find some shelter. When the storm stops, we'll search."

Reluctantly they continued.

15

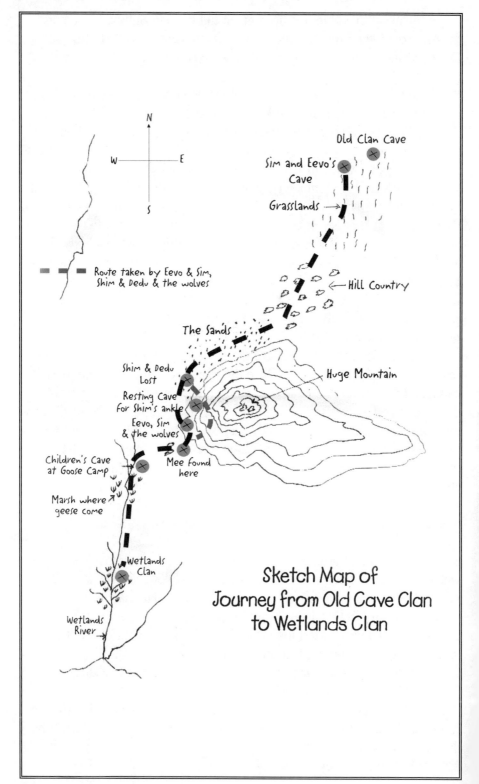

Sketch Map of
Journey from Old Cave Clan
to Wetlands Clan

Three

The Rescue

Unknown to the travellers, there were others who had been caught by the storm. A group of Wetlands hunters were out after the geese which came to the marshes every year. Once the weather in the lands where they spent the warm seasons became cold, these large birds headed south. The older geese were hard to catch, but this year's hatchlings could be snared fairly easily. Their flesh was more tender than that of the older birds. And so it was that the geese and hunters had this yearly meeting. Both came in response to the hunt for food — the geese for the grasses and seeds, the hunters for the geese, and everything else they could collect.

The hunters were accompanied by their mates, as there were many fruits and vegetables and seeds of grasses to gather as food for the coming cold time. The land about the streams and ponds that ran into the Wetlands river had much plant life with fruit now ripe. Once both the men and women came, they, of course, brought their children.

This year, the weather was not pleasant. It was cold and the wind blew steadily. It carried sand that stung when it hit faces, but it also brought in large flocks of storm-buffeted geese. Confused and not as wary as usual, the birds could easily be brought down the long sticks the hunters used. So despite the worsening weather, the hunt went on. In all the excitement, no one watched the sky.

The sandstorm hit suddenly. Visibility fell to zero. They were in a dense fog, not of water droplets but of stinging, blinding sand. Because the weather had been so foul, the children had been kept in a cave the hunters used when they stayed overnight. Even though the roar of the wind frightened them, and the younger ones were crying, none went outside. But as the storm continued, hunger added to their misery. The crying became louder. It was then that one little girl, decided to go and find her mother. No longer a toddler but a four-year-old, she considered herself quite capable. Out of the cave she went. Even though she knew where she wanted to go, the wind tossed her about. But there was no turning back. Reluctantly now, the little girl stumbled on for a very long time. Although she did not know it, she was in the low hills on the sunset side of the great mountain.

But it was becoming darker as the invisible sun dropped below the horizon. This was the time the predatory animals started their hunt, but she had no knowledge of this danger. Hungry and very sleepy, she took shelter behind a large pile of rock and curled up, trying to keep warm. Suddenly, a movement not far away caught her attention. Something was there! Slowly it moved towards her. She was terrified! Where was her mother? Eyes glinted in the moonlight, which now and again broke through the haze of the storm. They moved closer. Bravely, she felt the ground around her. All that could be found was a fist-sized stone. Should she throw it? She knew she could not throw that far. Paralyzed by fear, the little girl could not move.

The lynx, always on the watch for its usual diet of hare and small rodents, had never hunted game as big as this. The size made him pause, but not for long. Its stalking continued. This was a young animal. So intent on watching what it now considered its prey, it failed to check its surroundings. Another pair of eyes were watching. Originally, these eyes had been focused on the child, while the brain that controlled them was pondering its next move. The arrival of the lynx had changed all that. With the lynx now the important target, there was no hesitation in what the next move was to be.

Just as the lynx was about to pounce on the little girl, something large hit it. Massive teeth clamped on its neck. It had only time to hiss before being picked up and shaken. With its neck broken and its spinal cord severed, it knew no more. Its attacker dropped the now-limp body, looked at the little girl, and sat down.

The child was too afraid to move or make any sound. Her knees trembled uncontrollably, but the large animal did not do anything but sit and look at her. She sat and looked back. Then the animal lifted its head and howled. The little girl's terror increased. But what could she do? In a few moments, there was an answering howl. The watching animal replied, then lay down, crossed its front legs and continued to look at her.

She was beginning to ache from keeping herself rigid. She just had to move. As she changed position, the animal's head came up and then down again. Feeling a little bolder, the girl wiggled to make herself more comfortable. Again nothing happened. She could not move further away from the animal, as the rock she had rested against was right behind her. Since her arm tucked under her body had gone to sleep, she moved it. In doing so, her hand moved toward the animal. A large paw reached out and touched her hand. She recoiled. The paw withdrew. Curious, she reached out again and again the paw met her hand. This time, she closed her hand on that hard rough paw. For a few moments they both stayed like that, then the animal rolled over on its back.

She could feel the heat of the animal's belly. It seemed so soft and warm and inviting. She was so cold. Now no longer so frightened, but still respectful, she inched her way closer.

When Eevo and Sim and Grosh arrived, she was asleep, curled up against Neeth's belly.

Higher up on the mountain slope, visibility was much better and the quarter moon provided some light. Sim and Eevo, exhausted from their struggles in the sandstorm, were on the verge of sleep when the first wolf howl came.

"That sounds like Neeth," exclaimed Eevo, sitting upright.

Then came the answering call from another location, followed almost at once by what Eevo thought was Neeth's call. Then came silence. They again drifted off to sleep.

They were wakened by Grosh, who was making excited little whines and whimpers. It was obvious that she wanted them to follow her. Taking their spears but leaving the water bag, they moved out after the wolf. She would run, then stop, waiting for them to catch up, indicating her impatience by making small straight-legged jumps up and down in the same place.

"Why is she so excited?" asked Eevo. "Can they have found Mother and Dedu?"

Grosh led them at a rapid pace and, after climbing a slope, they saw Neeth lying on her side, or so it seemed. She had seen them but stayed where she was. "What is wrong?" They hurried to her side. With the moon unobstructed by cloud cover, they got a glimpse of a small motionless child nestled in the warmth of Neeth's belly.

"What happened?" asked Sim. Eevo bent down to feel the child, who, at Eevo's touch, opened her eyes and said, "I'm Mee. What's your name?"

"Hello, Mee," responded a startled Eevo. "My name is Eevo. My brother is Sim. How did you get here? Where's your mother?"

"Don't know. The wind blew me. I couldn't stop. It pushed me and pushed me. I walked and walked and walked. Momma got lost far away. I don't know where she is. I'm hungry and cold." She looked at Eevo, not wanting them to go away. "The big animal came and caught and shook the bad animal that wanted to hurt me. It shook it so hard it stopped moving. I was afraid, but it didn't hurt me. Just made a loud noise and watched me. Then it rolled over. It felt so warm and I was so cold. It warmed me up the way Momma does when it is cold in our cave. It's a good animal. It stopped the bad one. It hasn't moved after the big one shook it. But it might. It's over there." Mee pointed to the lynx.

Seeing the lynx again, its expression frozen in a snarl which made it look alive, made her cry. Eevo picked her up and held her close.

"We'll take you to our fire and get you something to eat," she said softly. "After the wind stops, we'll try to find your mother."

"I'll take the lynx and skin it later," said Sim. "It would be a pity to waste such warm fur." He grasped one of the animal's hind legs and dragged it along the ground. They returned to their fire, added some wood and gave the child a strip of the smoked meat and some water. Sim cut some evergreen branches and made a bed for her. She drank, ate the meat and was asleep almost as soon as she lay down.

As soon as the storm in the sand land stopped, they were going to look for their mother and her mate who had got lost. Mee had not known it before, but it seemed that mothers get lost easily. Eevo (Mee now knew the name meant "fast runner") had told her that this was the second time that their mother and her mate had been lost. Once they found their mother, they would look for Mee's.

The second day, Grosh brought back a goose. Eevo plucked off the feathers and cut the goose open. The animal friends ate the insides, but Sim and Eevo had cut up the goose and put pieces of meat on sticks and put them over the fire. Mee had never seen a goose put on the fire and she was not sure that she would like it. But she was hungry and tried some. It tasted better than goose the way they had it at her cave. Maybe Sim could show her mother how. Her mother was alone, without a mate now. Someone said that a mountain had killed him. She could not understand how. She and mother always had enough food because their favourite person, Seer, told the hunters to give it to them.

Four

Lost and Found

Just sitting and waiting for the storm to end and being unable to do anything else encourages worry. Shim and Dedu had plenty of time to worry as the storm continued steadily for four days. Then, as inexplicably as it had begun, it stopped. There was a dead calm. The sky had now cleared and the last rays of the setting sun gave them an indication of their direction. Gratefully, they set out again. The sliver of moon had grown and provided light and the sky was beautiful. But Shim could only hobble slowly. The soft sand made walking difficult and her foot was still quite painful. Despite protesting that he not do it, Dedu picked her up and carried her on his back. But they could travel neither fast nor far.

"We must get out of this sand country as soon as possible," said Dedu. "Once the sun appears, travelling will be almost impossible."

"The sun has only just set, and by the position of the great mountain I know that we are almost at the beginnings of the Wetlands." Shim tried to encourage her mate. "We might find a cave. We could make camp and stay until my foot is better. We're in no danger, but I worry about Eevo and Sim."

"Where they are, I don't know," replied Dedu. "But I'm not concerned about those two," he continued, lying to himself. "With their wolves to help them, they can look after themselves. We need to go on.

21

It may not be far, but we have to travel it."

With the added weight of Shim, Dedu's feet sank deeper into the sand, making every footstep a struggle. But he was strong and, although slowed, he managed at a steady pace. Before the moon was directly overhead, the ground underfoot became firm. By the light of the quarter moon they could make out trees ahead. The sound of running water could be heard.

"Put me down," insisted Shim. "We can stay here for the rest of the night. Tomorrow we will find a cave."

"Good," said Dedu. "After we find our cave, I'll gather wood. You light a fire. Its smoke will make it easier for Sim, Eevo and the wolves to find us."

"You seem to be very certain that they will try to find us. If they were experienced hunters, I could understand. But even if they're as big as we are, they're still young children."

Dedu chuckled at her description. "I have hunted with Sim. Ab has with both of them. They are far better hunters than either of us. They'll treat the hunt for us as they would the hunt for any animal. And they will find us. They're probably out looking even now."

Even though there was no evidence of any dangerous animals about, they took turns sleeping and watching until dawn. They searched for a cave and right in a large mound of a limestone outcropping, they found a space. Shim lit a fire and they set down to wait.

At first light the next day, with a full water bag, Eevo and Sim, along with Mee, set out to try to retrace their steps, making long zigzag sweeps across the sands. They found nothing. That night on the sands was unbelievably cold. They all huddled together for warmth. The next day, about mid-morning, Grosh found something. She began to run in circles. Before long both wolves began to act as if they had a positive trail.

Eevo, Sim and Mee followed as quickly as they could. By noon, Sim could see the actual footprints as could Eevo. But there was only one set of prints. Large prints, the kind Dedu would make. What had happened to Mother? Eevo began to hope that these were footprints of some other hunter. The thought that something had happened to Mother was more than she could bear. Just as they left the sands, the footprints ended.

They were now in a well-watered land of many ponds and streams. But the wolves did not hesitate, for they had a scent to follow. As they approached a low rock face, they could see a column of smoke coming from what could be a cave. Dedu had not yet been successful in lighting a fire. Mother often did. Eevo and Sim, forgetting little Mee, began to run. The wolves, however, were first, already at the cave with Dedu standing at the entrance.

Shim could hear Eevo exclaiming, "What happened to Mother? We only saw one set of footprints."

"She hurt her foot. I had to carry her," said Dedu. "She's in the cave and fine. But it still hurts her to walk." In the midst of all the excitement, little Mee was ignored. Shim, suddenly seeing a little girl standing near the entrance to the cave, said. "Who is she?"

Eevo started to tell her when Shim asked, "Are you Kno's daughter? The little girl who calls herself Mee?"

"Yes," said Mee, "because I am Mee."

"When did you find her? How long has she been lost?" asked Mother.

"I wasn't lost," said Mee. "Momma was lost like you were. Sim and Eevo didn't find me. Wonderful Friend did, and shook the bad animal so that it was dead."

At this point both Dedu and Shim had to hear the whole story. Then Dedu asked why Mee's clan were so far from the clan lands. He was told that it was to get geese and vegetables and grains.

"It's the yearly goose hunt," he exclaimed. "I was on it last year. The women usually stay for a short time and then go home. The men stay on for a hand of days or more depending on how successful the hunt is. After a feast, they return with their game."

He turned to Mee. "Were you in a big cave?"

"Yes," answered Mee. "They put us all there. The weather was bad. They all cried when the big wind started. Everybody except me. I didn't cry." Then she added, "Well, only a little."

Eevo smiled. Giving Mee a little hug, she said, "You were very brave."

Shim, knowing that Kno would be most upset, said so. Perhaps, since the hunt area was so close, Mee could be taken back to her mother. But Dedu reminded them that it might be wise to keep some distance from their hunting camp because of the wolves. He suggested that Sim take only one. "Hunters who do not know about friendly wolves might attack them."

Sim had been quiet up to this point, "My plan is to wait out of sight of their hunters until Mee sees someone she knows. Then we could have her go to that person. I will wait until she is safely back with whoever it is."

Mee, who had been listening to all of this, said with alarm in her voice, "I don't want anyone hurting Wonderful Friend."

Sim smiled at her, "They won't. Here take the lynx fur — the one you call the bad animal. That way your mother will know that your story really happened."

"And tell her that Shim and her family will be coming soon so that she can tell Seer," said Shim.

Mee nodded. After having some meat she now liked so much, and a drink of water, she, Sim and Neeth set out to find the goose hunters.

During the storm, one by one the hunters and the women of the Wetlands group made their way back to the cave near the goose-hunting grounds. By the second day everyone was accounted for except for little Mee. Kno was frantic with worry, but here too, there was nothing that could be done until the storm ended.

On the evening of the fourth day, with the storm over, Kno intended to go to find her daughter. The hunt master persuaded her that it was useless for her to try on her own. He promised that, in the morning, he and his best tracker would try to find the girl. Kno should go home with the other women. She absolutely refused. Mee was only four years old and had now been lost for four days in the worst storm anyone could remember. There was no chance that she was still alive. But the hunter had promised that he and the tracker would do their best.

There was only one direction little Mee could be headed — the direction of the wind. So the hunters set out that way. They found where she had broken some twigs climbing down an embankment. They found a place she had stopped to pee, and then the place she had chosen to sleep. They also found a place where a wolf had been watching her. The wolf

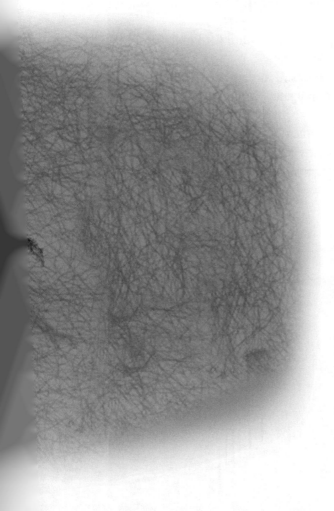

had been watching for a long time. Long enough for it to have urinated twice. Why would a wolf have waited so long before attacking? Attack it did. The places where its hind legs had torn the earth on its charge could clearly to be seen. Also visible were the drag marks where it had dragged the small body. Small blood stains had been left behind.

"I never would have thought she would have got so far," the tracker said. "Why did the wolf wait so long? It doesn't make sense. We have to tell Kno."

To their relief, Kno took the news calmly. She wanted to scream and shout and cry, but she did not do any of these. Instead, she left the cave and climbed a little knoll where she could be alone.

Little did she know that, a little higher up the slope, Sim and Mee and Neeth were watching. "That's my momma," said Mee to Sim." She looks sad."

"Run over to her," instructed Sim. "Neeth and I will stay here to make sure you're all right."

Mee started down the slope toward the knoll. As she came closer, she called out. "Momma, Momma."

Kno looked up. Her desire for her little one was making her ears play tricks. Then she heard it again. "Momma, Momma." She looked around. Coming down from the higher ground, she saw Mee. It couldn't be! But ghost or apparition, she didn't care. She ran from the knoll toward what looked like her daughter. The "Momma, wait till I tell you what happened to me" was too real not to be true.

Sim and Neeth turned back towards the cave.

Five

Not Welcome

After waiting about two hands of days, Shim felt that her ankle was well enough to continue her trip. They set out, following the stream that ran out of the pond near the cave until it joined a small river, which in turn joined a larger one. Dedu recognized the river. This was the way they had come, some three hands of moons ago, on their first trip to find Seer, Shim's father.

By mid-afternoon they reached the wetlands. Before them loomed a large cliff, and in this cliff face were many cave openings set at various levels. These openings were joined one to the other by narrow paths. Fairly low on the cliffside were a number of large caves, the largest of which was the Flint Works Cave. This is where Seer lived and worked. Despite the size of the clan, all was peaceful.

"This clan is even bigger than your description of it," said Sim, awestruck as he looked up at the tier upon tier of caves.

With the arrival of Shim and her family, that peace of the place was shattered. Confusion broke out among the first people to see the wolves.

"Wolves are coming!" someone shouted. The cry of alarm was taken up by others. Quickly a group of armed men arrived. Dedu and Shim were also shouting, trying to prevent the spearing of Neeth and

Grosh. Fortunately, one of the hunters recognized Dedu as a hunting companion, and tried to halt the attack. Unfortunately, his words were not heard in the confusion that followed. Some hunters at the rear surged forward. One of them was shouting, "Kill the wolves!" He pulled back his arm and was about to spear Grosh. Only Sim's and Eevo's spears stopped him. The situation was tense. These men, all of them good hunters, had organized themselves to protect their homes from any danger. To them, wolves were an enemy to be destroyed.

What might have happened next is not known since the hunt leader arrived precisely at this time. Right away he knew Dedu. He ordered his men to stop. What was going on? Someone could be hurt.

"Call Seer," Shim shouted. But before Seer could get there, Mee, pushing her way through the forest of adult legs, ran up to Neeth and hugged her around the neck. Grosh came up and sat down beside her. Mee turned on the hunters and said, "Leave my Wonderful Friend alone! Don't hurt Watchful either." Looking right at the hunt leader she said, "Wonderful Friend found me and killed the bad animal."

At first the Hunt Leader looked astonished, then he let out a great laugh. "Put up your spears," he said to the armed group. "These wolves are friends to people." Turning to the tracker standing beside him, he exclaimed, "That explains it! The wolf was her guardian. Now it becomes clear. No wonder that wolf was there so long. She was watching Mee and waiting for the two young people. She has talked so much about 'Wonderful Friend,' I thought she meant the young man."

Just then Seer arrived. He stared in surprise, then walked over to the group, unaware of what had happened. "You're back!" He greeted Shim and Dedu warmly, then turned toward Eevo and Sim. He looked at them, a smile on his face. "I'm delighted. You've brought the children as you promised. You two, I know are Eevo and Sim. You, Eevo, I would recognize anywhere. You look just like your mother did when I lost her many years ago." He approached Sim to make him feel welcome. "I feel I know you from what Shim and Dedu have told me. You are just the person I've been waiting for."

Suddenly, he caught sight of the two wolves sitting quietly by Eevo's feet. He looked at them with interest. "Now could you introduce me to your two other friends? It seems that you've done something I always thought possible. I just never have a chance to try. Did you find then when they were very small?"

"Yes," replied Eevo. "Their mother was injured by hyenas. Sim fought and killed the one that had wounded her. She was badly hurt and died three days later. We took the cubs back to our cave. They were only one or two moons old. We fed them eggs and a little meat. Since then we've lived together. Now they're part of our family."

She went up to Seer and said, "May I?" Eevo took his hand and led him to Grosh who smelled the hand and then pushed her head against Seer's leg. Seer was next introduced to Neeth in exactly the same way, in full view of all the people who just a short time ago were trying to kill the wolves. For many, this new development was hard to accept, but they respected Seer, the elder in their clan.

Now that peace had been restored, Seer led his family into the Flint Works Cave, where he now spent most of his time. Once inside, Seer asked, "Did you have any trouble crossing the sands? I'm glad that you didn't come about three hands of days earlier. We had a terrible windstorm. No one out on the sands could have survived it."

"We were caught in it," Dedu said. "We were already crossing the sands when it started." He went on to tell about Shim's ankle and their being separated, right up to Sim and Eevo finding Mee with the wolf. Sim described taking the child to her mother, but not entering the hunt camp because of the wolves. "We spent another two hands of days waiting for Shim's foot to improve. Today we made our way here."

"But what did you do for water during and after the storm?" asked Seer. "I just don't know how you survived."

"We had a good supply of water," Shim continued the story. She brought out the bags, the ones Sim had suggested be made. Seer looked at them and then at Sim. He looked at the spear that Sim was carrying and the axe that hung over Dedu's shoulder.

"Did Sim also make these?" he asked. "Tell me all about it."

The story of what had happened while Dedu and Shim had been away visiting Seer was recounted. As the story unfolded, Seer became ever more impressed.

"It is given to some people to find one or, if very fortunate, perhaps two truths," he said, "but you two between you have uncovered so many. I thought that I would teach you, Sim, but it is I who will have to learn. I can help you especially in working with flint. I can give you some of what I have learned, from others and from my experience — things that age has taught me. Other than that I can only say that you, the two of you, have changed the ways that people will live.

"Eevo, your discovery of how a fire can be created is probably the most important discovery ever made. As for the wolves, I have dreamed about something like that, people and clever animals becoming one family. That partnership may be as important as fire."

Six

Seer, The Elder

A creative person! Seer could hardly believe his good fortune — and his daughter's son! He needed to see more.

"Now, Sim, I want to see your knives and spears. But first I really need to see that axe."

Seer examined the weapon and its bindings. He checked the ridged, sharpened edges and the feel of the axe in his hand. "Very good," he concluded. "Now let me see your spears and knives." Seer examined each with great care, then turned to Sim and asked, "How did you break your flint stones to make your edges? The points of the spears are all sharp but of different shapes and sizes. You've done well to make such useful instruments, but I can show you how to make them so that they are more alike. Your spears will have better balance and, although not as sharp, the points will last far longer. Did you just break the flint and use the sharp fragments? That's what I did, always bruising and cutting my hands."

Sim laughed and admitted to doing just that. He told how in frustration he finally broke his first flint by hurling it against a rock. Seer said that he had broken his by putting it on a flat rock and then hitting it with another flint piece. Both had shattered, leaving him with some pieces he could use. How proud he was then to have done so!

"After I had my sharp fragments, I went to a clan near the one where I was born. There I learned from their old flint worker by watching him. He taught me something about flint knapping. Now you too have come to an old flint worker. We tool-makers must pass on our skills to those who come after us. What made you try to make tools?"

Sim knew he had found a teacher, someone he could talk with and share ideas. "We needed a knife. I knew a little about it from the knife Dedu used, the one you made for Mother many years ago. I tried to imitate it but couldn't. But I did get three sharp-edged pieces that could be used for cutting. When my fire-hardened spears did not penetrate the skins of some of the animals we were hunting, I knew that the tips had to be sharper. Because I had knives, I could shape the spear shafts from straight dry wood, instead of just using saplings. I could make notches to hold the flint heads. Once I tied the heads on tightly with wet rawhide, I had a spear."

"That's it exactly!" exclaimed Seer. "One tool leads to another."

Before leaving the cave with Sim to find some hammer stones, Seer checked his supply of flint cores. He found one about the size of a human head. Sim had never imagined using a flint stone as large as that. But he noticed Seer was having difficulty finding things in the dark corners of his cave. Sim was concerned. How could he bring some light inside?

"This is exactly what we want," said Seer, noting Sim's look of astonishment at the size of the flint. "Small pieces are far harder to work with. This will break to give us good flakes. Watch this."

Taking a piece of leather and folding it into a pad to protect his thigh, Seer placed the flint against the pad. Then, taking his hammer stone, he hit the flint at an angle. A large flake of flint, about the size of an oak leaf and as thick as one's finger, sheered off. The break left a smooth, slightly concave surface. Again he struck off another flake much the same size and shape as the first.

Seer then held up the first leaf-shaped flake. He chipped away at its edges and, almost magically, a well-shaped spearhead appeared. Using a piece of antler, he pushed off tiny flakes at the lower edges of the flint flake, creating two notches that would make binding to a spear shaft extremely easy.

"This is a crude but useful spear point," said Seer.

"Crude?" wondered Sim. It was beautiful! He realized that he had far to go before he could do work that Seer did so easily.

Seeing Sim's awe, Seer said, "Before two moons have passed you will be making far better ones. I have looked at your work. You have learned the important part. Now I will show you how you can make it better. Remember, your spears have worked very well. During the hunt, the appearance doesn't matter, how well it works does."

As Sim followed the wolves and Seer out of the cave, he noticed that the wolves seemed to accept Seer as much as they had Mother. They acted as if they knew Seer. Here was a puzzle, something that he would have to think about. What was so familiar about Seer? It wasn't just the wolves. Sim felt it too. Somehow he felt that he had always known this man he had just met. He would have to ask Eevo to see if she too felt the same way.

Seven

Fire Making

They returned to the cave entrance to find Dedu talking to a group of men.
Most of them did not believe his story of the tiger war. He was getting a
little upset and wanted Sim to explain. But before Sim could begin to
speak, Seer took over. Everyone in that clan took Seer's words as true. He
was their wise man. Older than any person anyone knew, he seemed to
know everything. They felt lucky to have him as their elder.

Seer began by saying, "The stories you will hear about these two
young people will be hard to believe, but they are true. They have done
things that have never been done before. What would we do if we had a
storm of driving rain, and all the clan fires had been put out?"

One of the hunters answered, "We would send a group of hunters
to the people who live by the salt water. We would ask them for a new
fire. We would have to send some knives and spears to pay for the fire."

"Is there no other way? If we lost our fires, they very likely would
also have lost theirs," Seer reminded them. "Then what would we do? But
today, with these two young people and their hunt helpers, the wolves, we
are fortunate. Now we do not have to send anyone anywhere."

Seer turned to Eevo. "Will you show the people of this clan the
wonderful gift you have brought. Then tell them how you discovered the
gift of fire making. Tell them how you promised the Sun that you would

teach it to all people."

Eevo looked around her, startled by the request. There were so many people. They were all looking at her. Could she do it? "Yes, she could," she told herself.

Eevo smiled and took out her fire-making tools. She crushed some dry shreds of grass and some wood shavings to make some tinder. Kneeling on the ground, she was about to start when she remembered Ab and his way of asking for the Sun's help. Eevo stood erect, faced the light and raised her arms up toward the Sun, making a gesture of request. Then, placing the fire board on the ground, Eevo began to twirl the rubbing stick between her hands, holding it firmly against the fire board. As she was now a capable fire maker, a wisp of smoke soon arose. Then came the glowing ember, which she carefully slid into her prepared dry tinder. Gently, she blew it into a flame. She added a little more tinder and placed the fire into the bed of dry wood that Sim had prepared. Soon a brisk fire was going. The crowd around her had increased as she worked. Now a chorus of voices shouted their delight and wonder at what they had seen.

"Now, do any of you doubt what you have heard about these two?" Seer continued. "Eevo discovered the secret of fire making. Sim developed the tools to make it easy. That means most people can make fire. Sim, with no instruction to guide him, figured out how to make good flint and wood tools. Eevo, not yet a full woman, worked out the plan for chasing the great sabre-toothed tiger away. Between the two of them, they befriended the wolves and became one clan with them. Each one of those four, the two wolves and Eevo and Sim, does the thing that each can do best. Together they solve the problems facing them. It is good for us that they are here."

Seer stopped talking, wanting to make sure that everyone was understanding him. Seemingly satisfied, he continued, "My vision is failing me where I need it most, for close-up work. Sim is young. Soon he will be making tools that I believe will be better than mine. We already have a good and well-fed clan here. But now I can see our life becoming better."

Eleven-year-old Sim enjoyed the praise. But at the same time, it embarrassed him. He knew his tools would never be better than Seer's. He would consider himself lucky if they were as good. When he looked at Eevo, he saw that her face was flushed too. Even Dedu and Shim looked at them both with pride. Watching Seer, he suddenly knew why he felt he knew him. Seer's way of talking and the way he moved and used his hands were just like Mother's, and to a great degree like Eevo's. The wolves must have sensed that too. That would explain their confusion on meeting Mother and now their acceptance of Seer. Why would that be?

By now Eevo had a crowd around her. Everyone wanted to see the tools that made fire. She told how she had reasoned that the fire was trapped in the wood, that fire really was that bit of itself that the Sun put into all living things. And that this fire could be released by rubbing, since rubbing, if fast enough, would make the wood hot. If the two pieces rubbed together were both of wood, and the rubbing was very fast, and there was no time to cool the rubbed surfaces, the heat produced would be enough to let out the fire trapped inside. That way it could escape to the outside and rejoin the Sun.

Eevo showed them again by lighting another fire. She told again of her promise to the Sun, and how she had trained Ree and Ur as "Keepers of the Fire" at her home clan. She would teach them how to make fire.

Seer said this was a good idea. He suggested that everyone interested should look at Eevo's fire-making wood, then go out and find their own fire-starting tools. This would help them if they were away from the caves and needed to make a fire. He also asked all hunters to spread the word to other hunters from other clans. Tell them that a young woman, chosen by the Sun to teach people the secret of fire making, was here. All who wanted to learn were welcome at the caves of the Wetlands Clan. Turning to Eevo, he said that she would be busy for as long as she wanted, spreading the Sun's message to all people. He said that so important a calling required a special cave for its purpose. It should be called the Cave of the Sun. The cave that got the light of the morning sun and one that was higher than most would be ideal.

By now the sun was low on the horizon. As this was the time the wolves liked to hunt for themselves, they left to explore their new territory. Sim, Eevo, Shim, Dedu and Seer went back to Seer's cave. One of the women would be coming soon with food for him, some dried fish and tubers.

"Would you like to try some of the food we brought with us to use on our trip?" asked Shim. "It is different from the food here. I think you will like it." She unwrapped a bundle of the smoked meat.

"Whatever that is, it does smell good," said Seer, "Please let me see it." He picked up a strip of meat and felt it, tore off a small piece and then smelled it.

"By its look, it must be from a large animal. Something strange has been done to it. It is not simply dried, because it bends easily. Its smell tells me that fire was used to change it. Let me taste it."

Eevo described the accidental roasting of the rabbit. Because they had liked the taste so much, they began to suspend their meat on sticks over the fire. Sometimes the meat would burn, so they tried longer sticks as spits. Every so often they would leave the meat overnight over a fire that had green wood put on it to slow the rate of burning. These fires would smoke a lot. The meat, and especially the fish, would develop the smell and taste of the smoke. Everyone who tried it liked that taste and, since it allowed the meat to keep for many days, they began to use smoke rather than just drying to preserve meat and fish.

"So you see, it was all an accident and not something we did!" added Eevo.

"The first time was an accident, the rest was deliberate," Seer reminded her.

"Now what is the meat?" he asked. "It tastes very good. But what animal is it from? That I can't identify."

"Elk," said Sim, "One of those giant deer. The bone hammer you use for finishing your flints came from the antler of one of those."

"You know how to get that kind of horn?" Seer was surprised. "I got the one I have many, many years ago. They are very difficult to get. Our hunters seldom see any of those animals. And when they do, they can't get near enough to kill them."

"We have killed two," said Sim. "The real reason for that last hunt was because we needed the large stomach and bladder for our water bags. With the help of the wolves, elk are really quite easy to hunt."

Sim had been watching Seer closely. He added, "As soon as I saw you, Seer, I felt that I had always known you. The wolves acted as if they did too. Wolves do not make friends easily, except with children and then only with very young ones. But they let you touch them right away. And they touched you. Now that I have watched you and heard you talk, I realize that you and Mother and Eevo move and talk much the same way. Can that be the reason? Does anyone know why?"

No one, not even Seer, had any answers. He said that he, too, had a feeling that Sim and Eevo were people he knew, but had thought that it was because they had been described to him.

Soon, tired after such a busy day, they all went to sleep.

Eight

Changes

Life with the Wetlands Clan was good, but it was different. Now that they were part of a much larger group of people, this meant some changes in their way of living. Most were for the better, but there was one thing in particular that Eevo and Sim missed. Their cave had a pool of cool spring water. But here, bathing was more difficult. The others only washed infrequently, if at all, and the smell was most unpleasant. Whenever possible, Eevo and Sim avoided going into the common caves. Not being able to bathe before sleeping began to bother them. Although the river was close at hand, it was a fairly large rushing stream. Entering it in the dark was not wise.

Feeling desperate, Sim suddenly thought of the curve in the river where he had gone with Seer to get hammer stones. Could this provide a bathing spot? He called Eevo and the two went to explore the bend at the point where the river became shallow on the outside of the big sweep to the right. Just upstream was a large boulder blocking the flow of the river; however, the water was deep and fast as it swept around this rock. Bathing there would be dangerous.

As the days shortened more and the cold season arrived, they used their shallow bathing place less and less. Sim continued to explore the bend in the river, looking at the area from every which way. Just what he wanted to do he did not know, but something in his mind kept coming back to that river bend. One day while sitting on a rock and thinking, he began to scratch in the sand with his digging stick. He looked at the scratches and at the river and back at his marks in the sand. Suddenly he became aware of what he had been doing; he had made something to show the river as it was. Quickly he made a few more lines to show some changes. Maybe they could change the path of the water. "Those lines in the sand help thinking a lot," he muttered to himself. Sim paused to look at what he had done. "That's it!" he exclaimed. "That's how we can do it!"

Sim ran back to get Eevo and Seer. "Come and see!" he yelled. Shim and Dedu heard the noise and came too. What could be making Sim so excited?

"These scratches show the river at this place," Sim explained. "Now look. What would happen if we dig around that huge stone and if we put more rocks on either side of it? Perhaps the water would pass on the other side of the boulder. That would make this bend in the river almost like a closed pond. With only a little water coming through, the water would become much warmer. Wouldn't that make a safe place for everybody to bathe?"

Seer was very impressed by the idea, but even more impressed by the sketch Sim had made. What a wonderful way to help thinking! "I have never thought of that. It is very clever and, now that he has done it, so obvious," he thought to himself.

"But you know we can't do it," said Eevo. "Who would do all that digging? We would need all the people in the clan to help. I don't think they would be willing."

Sim was ready with an answer. "I've thought about that. I think the water will help us. All we need to do is dig a small ditch from the lower end of the bend, around the other side of the boulder to the upper part of the bend. Once we get water flowing, we can keep scraping the channel deeper. The water flow will carry the soil downstream."

"Well, I don't know," said Eevo, not yet convinced. "But maybe, if it would only need the two of us. Perhaps some of the children would help if we can turn it into a game."

Every day, whenever they had some time, the two, with considerable help from Dedu and a few of the younger children, worked. They scraped out dirt, pulled out shrubs and moved rocks to make their ditch. Just as the cold season ended, they broke through from one part of the bend to the other. The water started to move in the ditch. At first it was only a trickle, but soon a regular fast stream was flowing. With the warmer weather, the snow in the mountains melted and the river became higher.

40

Now it was no longer necessary to try to deepen the trench. The fast-flowing water did their work for them. The river had lost its obstruction and was flowing on a straight course. Where the bend had been was a large pond with an inlet from the upper part of the river and an outlet to the lower part of the river. The water would stay clean and fresh.

With the pond made, Eevo and Sim and the children rushed in to try it. Even Dedu went in up to the depth of his thigh, but only to wash the mud off his legs, he said. Now the clan had a safe place where even young ones could go in the water. Those who had worked on the construction used it regularly. Then, one by one, parents came to see what their children were doing. Some stayed to try the pond. Many returned and brought others. Gradually, the people were becoming cleaner and, better yet, they were enjoying it.

Originally Sim had thought he would be spending almost all of his time becoming a better flint worker. That is not how it worked out. First there was the pond making, which took a lot of time. And now many members of the clan, who in the past would have asked Seer for help in various projects, were now asking him to help solve some problem or other.

Eevo needed fire boards. She and Father had found some of the right kind of wood, a dry dead tree. But unlike the wood at the old cave site, this had not been split by a landslide. Much work was required to make it right. One day Eevo brought in a small log about as long as a person's forearm from finger tips to elbow, and about as thick as a person's thigh. Father had chopped this section off from one of the larger branches, but his axe was not able to split it into flat pieces. She wanted boards that would be thin and flat. Flat was important to prevent rolling when the fire stick was being twirled rapidly. And it had to be thin. Experience had taught her that if the fire board was thick, it was much harder to get the wood to heat enough to produce an ember.

All three of them, Eevo, Seer and Sim, examined the problem. The wood was from one of the evergreen type of trees with flat needle leaves. Many of these trees were growing in the wetlands. They had egg-shaped cones with rather smooth scales. Blisters in the smooth bark contained a very sticky gum that was useful for covering cuts.

"I know that wood well," Seer noted. "I have often used that gum to cover wounds. Because it is sticky, I have used it to join flint spearheads to the shafts before tying them in. The wood is soft and splits easily."

Sim had no idea how flat boards could be made. The tree he had used had been crushed in a landslide. Seer showed him how a flint wedge could be used. With Eevo helping him, he split the log in two. Then, using the wedge again, he split off another flat piece, and another. These needed only a little trimming to be ready for use. It was all so simple that Sim was a bit ashamed that he had not thought of it himself.

Later that day, Dedu came in to the Flint Works Cave. He wanted three axes and five spears. A hunt was to be organized. The clan hunters wanted to try to get some of the horses often found coming to the river to drink. Dedu would go with them. Later one of the clan hunters arrived. The bindings that held his spearhead to the shaft had become loose. Could Sim repair it? Sim could and did.

Finally, Sim was free of tasks. He began to cut pieces of chalk he had found in Seer's collection of stones. Chalk is a very soft stone that splits easily but tends to crumble if one is not careful. He cut each piece into a more or less shape of a cube, about a hand's length on each side. When he had made four, he began to chip out a hollow in each one, about a thumb's measure deep.

Seer watched him. And as Sim did not say what he was making, Seer commented, "Those are a little small for water containers. It seems that you are not saying what they're for. Perhaps I have to wait to see."

Sim grinned and said nothing. He had a supply of liquid fat in one of Seer's fire pots. It had become a custom that whenever meat and fish were roasted on spits over the fire, the fat drippings, as much as possible, were collected and stored. Fat that dripped into the fire caused flare-ups and burned. That which landed in the ashes made a sticky, smelly mess that required cleaning.

That evening, as they all sat about the fire at the entrance to Seer's cave, Sim left the group and went inside. He filled the hollows in his four chalk containers with the liquid fat. Then he placed a twist of the fibrous strands that Mother was collecting for her rug weaving into the oily liquid. He placed three of the containers around the work site and carried the fourth one to the fire. Sim then lit the wick. A pleasant, steady light glowed, creating light in the area where the family group was sitting. Seer stroked his beard and grinned.

"A light!" he exclaimed. "That casts light on what you were doing this afternoon." The others all laughed.

"Well done, Sim," said Shim. "I'm glad that I didn't say anything about not having lamps here as we did at the other cave. It would have spoiled the surprise. Let me show show what I've been doing."

She produced a mat made of rushes held together by many strands of cord. The mat could be rolled up or folded and stayed together as one piece. All were delighted.

42

"It took a long time to make and it will make a good sleeping mat. But I need a simpler, easier way of twisting the fibers into cord."

"It's well-made," observed Seer. "There may be no easier way."

"I will try to find an easier way," said Eevo. "It looks like fun, but not tonight."

It had been a good day. Now, as usual, the wolves got up and left for their evening hunt. The humans went to sleep, Shim curled up on her new mat.

Nine

Hyenas

Life in the Wetlands Clan went on much as usual despite the newcomers. Having strangers who were not really strangers was good for everyone. While there was some worry about the presence of the wolves, especially by the mothers of young children, the children themselves, especially Mee, were delighted.

Mee, now about five years old, had decided from the beginning that the wolves were there to be her playmates. After all, they had been friends since Neeth had found her. Frequently, she could be found waiting outside Seer's cave for the wolves to come out to play. And play they did. The wolves treated the small children the way they instinctively treat cubs, accepting all kinds of torture the little ones inflicted. Mee, as the eldest of the young children, ran the show. Although the mothers were not altogether happy, the children almost always seemed to find ways to slip away. Soon the whole group became the best of friends.

With the cold weather period came the usual decrease in the length of days. Here in the wetlands there was little snow and none of the food shortages that the smaller, or more poorly located, clans experienced. A full year and perhaps two moons had passed. Sim was now nearly twelve years old and taller now than even Eevo, far taller than anyone in the clan. No one even paid any attention to his club foot any more.

By now a pattern of activities had been set. Shim was busy weaving rugs as well as looking after the ailments and wounds that occurred in the clan. Eevo taught fire making to the clan people, but now had less to do because few visitors came during the cold weather since the mountain passes were blocked by snow. Dedu had become the hunt master of large animal hunts for the clan, the same position that he had held back in his own clan.

Dedu was not fond of fish. Goose was all right, but sometime it tasted rather fishy, so he had organized some very successful hunts for the only large grasseater to be found in the area, the horse. Large herds of these smallish animals could be found and since they had not been hunted before, they were easy to approach. Sim, under Seer's guidance, had become an expert worker in flint and was now also making wonderfully sharp long-bladed knives from a beautiful black stone, found on the slopes of the old fire mountains.

Because the wetlands was an excellent source of good food, this clan had many more people than Dedu's group. More people meant there were also more children. And, of course, the presence of helpless young of any species meant that there always predators prowling nearby. Because of this, the children were always warned to stay close to their mothers. But, even so, every few months in the past a child would be carried off or badly hurt. The chief predator as always was the hyena. However, for the past year this had not happened as Neeth and Grosh had kept predators away.

Recently, however, a new pack of hyenas, with about fourteen members, had moved into the area. Because of its size, this pack, under the leadership of an experienced female, was quite aggressive. A number of times they had come near the Wetlands caves, but there were always too many of the big two-legged animals about for them to raid. This day, having spotted a number of young together, they may have felt that there was a good chance of picking up one or two. Because hyenas are intelligent creatures, they do not run in and attack at once. Instead they consider the possibility of danger, and circle their prey to drive them in the direction they want them to go. They began to circle the children. Very quickly the little ones realized that these were not friendly animals. Frightened, they began to cry and huddle together. Mee started yelling, "Neeth! Grosh!"

Sim at work, flaking a spearhead, thought he heard something faintly in the distance. But when both wolves, who had seemed to be napping, exploded out of the cave, he knew that something was wrong. As he rushed out, he could smell the powerful odour of hyena. Grabbing a spear and telling Seer that hyenas were close by, he raced after the wolves.

46

Dedu, who was with Eevo watching Shim weave another sleeping mat, also heard the child. Recognizing the note of fear in the call, he too started to run, closely followed by both Eevo and Shim. As Eevo passed the mouth of the cave, she grabbed two of the spears from the stack leaning against the wall.

The wolves got there first. They tore into the circle of hyenas. Immediately, two hyenas were lying out of action, hamstrung by the wolves on their first rush. The rest of the pack, falling back slightly, turned on the wolves. The wolves did not even pause. They were defending their cubs and in such a situation would fight to their death. Neeth knocked over one and quickly tore its throat out. Grosh snapped the tendons on another hyena's hind leg. Now Sim's spear accounted for one. Then Dedu's axe quickly dispatched two more. The remaining hyenas left the fight, snarling as they retreated. Shim and Eevo killed the three crippled hamstrung ones. Ordinarily, that should have been the end of the battle, the hyenas retreating and the others breaking off the fight. But this time, Sim gave the wolves the signal, which meant, "Herd the hunted animals." The wolves were only too glad to do so.

By now the other clan hunters had responded to the danger. And by the time they arrived, they saw something they had never imagined possible. Seven hyenas were lying dead, seven others were trying to retreat but were being driven back toward the four humans who killed two, one after the other. The other five barely managed to escape. Just moments after the attack had begun, a pack of fourteen hyenas had been reduced to five survivors. The wolves and people had suffered no injuries. If any confirmation of the truth of the tiger war was needed, this episode provided it. Any secret doubt among the clan hunters was gone.

Mee looked at everyone and laughed. She hugged Neeth and Grosh in turn, and had her face licked and covered with hyena blood from Neeth's muzzle. Her mother, distressed at the thought of what had almost happened, went to the wolves and thanked them as she would have people. Any concerns the people of the clan may have had about wolves living among them was now completely put to rest. The wolves were honoured members of the clan.

Ten

Wolves

As the cold months grew to a close, wolf howls in the distance were heard more frequently. The behaviour of Neeth and Grosh changed. They became restless and howled in answer. People began to worry as this had never happened before. Even Sim and Eevo, who knew the wolves very well, were a little disturbed by their restlessness. Dedu, as an experienced hunter, was aware that this type of wolf behaviour was not uncommon. But for the Wetlands, this was much more than usual wolf activity. It was happening much closer to the caves and seemed to involve Grosh and Neeth. However, it was Seer who was the first to say anything reasonable.

"Neeth and Grosh are full grown now," he said. "They are getting to the time when they will want the companionship of other wolves. Sometimes when I have difficulty sleeping, I can hear them outside talking to wolves. Some members of a wolf pack can be heard quite close to the caves during the night." Seer showed his concern. "We have never had any problems with wolves attacking any of our people, but many people fear them. After what Neeth and Grosh have done for us, no one will say anything against them. But a hidden fear of strange wolves is still there."

"The two are now wanting cubs of their own," Shim observed. "Look how they treat the very young children. That's it! Those strange wolves we hear must be male wolves who can smell that our two are ready to mate."

That evening after the wolves had gone out, Sim picked up a spear and stepped out. "Don't go alone." Dedu warned. "When strange things occur it can be dangerous. I will come with you."

The two of them tried to follow Neeth and Grosh, but they did not want to be trailed. Experienced trackers that they were, Sim and Dedu still lost them. Only once did they get a glimpse of a shadowy wolf figure. Frustrated, they returned home.

Three days later the wolves left in the evening as usual, but did not return next morning. Two more days passed and still there was no sign of them. Even more disturbing to Sim, the wolf howls had stopped. Eevo, somewhat alarmed, nevertheless was calm. "They're very capable of looking after themselves," she reminded Sim. "When they have finished doing whatever they set out to do, they'll be back. Really, there is nothing we can do."

When three more days had passed with no sign of either wolf, Sim packed a pouch with dried smoked meat. He strapped a spear and the partly filled small water bag on his back, carried another spear in his hand, and set out to try to search. Perhaps he could convince Grosh and Neeth to come back with him. After all, they were his young sisters. He and Eevo had raised them. For two days he explored the area in vain. There was no sign that there had ever been any wolves. Finally, tired and discouraged, Sim came back. Nothing the others did could lift his mood. Nothing interested him. Often he could be found, just sitting and staring off into space.

For some time Neeth and Grosh had been trying to meet the wolves that had been calling to them. Those wolves were shy. But there was one female wolf that would chase them off before either Neeth or Grosh make contact. One evening, tired of this calling, then running away, they followed the wolves back to their pack territory, but did not enter. The area was well marked by the Alpha male and some instinct told them to stay out. Establishing themselves just outside of the pack boundary, they settled down to watch.

Both Grosh and Neeth were now fully mature and both were ready to mate. The male wolves who could smell them were getting excited, even the Alpha male. The Alpha female, however, was annoyed and angry. She would chase and nip the younger males, and even her mate. She would have liked to chase the two strange females away, but here too, wolf instincts prevented her from doing so. The two were not in the territory she could defend.

By now some six days had passed. Neeth and Grosh were becoming more and more frustrated at this stand-off. It was not only the males who were excited. Neeth and Grosh were watching the male wolves and smelling the urine they were depositing in copious quantity. Feeling a strange urging they had never experienced before, they broke the taboo and entered the pack's territory. This was just the opportunity the Alpha female needed. Once they crossed into pack territory, she charged towards them, fangs bared. She and her mate were the dominant wolves of the pack, and it was she, and only she, in this pack who would have cubs. Now here were two intruding females ready to mate. Confident in her territorial rights, she felt that she had wolf custom on her side. A determined attack by her would drive these two interlopers away.

Had she been dealing with wolves from another pack, this would probably have been true. But Neeth and Grosh had changed; no longer did they totally follow wolf-pack behaviour. They were not prepared to accept her authority. Eevo and Sim were their pack leaders. From their earliest days, they had never experienced times of starvation. Eevo and Sim had rescued them, fed them, then hunted with them. Consequently, they were far bigger than the average wolf. Having always worked together, they knew what the other was thinking. Never in a subservient position, they were not going to allow some bossy female wolf to intimidate them. This Alpha female had no chance.

Suddenly she was on her back with two large wolves, canine teeth bared, standing over her. In an instance she had lost her Alpha status. Her mate, quickly sizing up the situation, felt that it would be folly to come to her assistance. Fearfully, she accepted the dominance of the two strangers and whimpered. It was only then that Grosh and Neeth let her up. She, with tail between her legs, slunk away. They ignored her mate, the male Alpha, but chose the two three-year-old males, the ones who had been calling to them, and cut them out of the pack, just as they had done to horses in the past, following direction from Dedu.

The four left the pack, much to the relief of the female leader and her mate. He, for one, was glad to get rid of two offspring. Soon they would have challenged him and each other for the pack leadership. Neeth and Grosh now spend some time establishing their dominance over these two young males and, when they were satisfied, took them back to the Wetlands caves.

One evening, Sim was watching from his lookout. Lately he had spent most of his time scanning the horizon for his wolf friends. This night he fell asleep and, in a fitful dream, thought he felt something cold pushing under his sleeping fur. Something was blowing on the back of his neck. Reaching over in his mostly asleep state to pull up his fur cover, he felt a cold muzzle and a warm licking tongue. Suddenly awake, he sat upright and put his arms around a familiar furry neck. Grosh was back. He hugged that well-known friendly form and began to cry, his body wracked with great sobs. Silently Neeth appeared. With his sobs now under control, Sim stood up.

Neeth took Sim's hand in her mouth and began to lead him to the edge of the rocky ledge, the boundary of the caves. Sitting there were two other wolves. One growled when Sim, pulled by Neeth, came close. That growl ended in a sharp yelp as Grosh nipped that wolf. One at a time the two wolves were pushed up and made to acknowledge Sim. It was a ceremony much like the one when Seer was introduced to Neeth and Grosh. Sim sat down and waited. Slowly, first one and then the other wolf came forward. When Sim stretched out his hand, the first wolf stepped back and showed his teeth. A growl from both Grosh and Neeth stopped that behaviour instantly. Gently, Sim touched the trembling wolf. Gradually, as the human fingers touched the its head and ears, then scratched its head, the wolf relaxed. The second wolf, seemingly having observed what happened, was more co-operative. Touching him was easier. Sim then tried to lead all four to his lookout, the two males requiring some persuasion. Once there, all five sat down and waited for the rosy signs of dawn.

Eevo woke first and glanced over to Sim's sleeping mat. Sim was not there. It looked as if he had not been there all night. "I hope he has not gone off again looking for the wolves," thought Eevo. "Can he still be up on that rock?"

Not waiting for the others to wake, she left the cave and began to climb toward the lookout. Some movement appeared to be there. She looked again and saw a wolf. It was not either Neeth or Grosh. Not being armed, Eevo stopped abruptly. To her relief, Neeth's head appeared, then Grosh. The two sisters came bounding down to greet her. Looking up for Sim, Eevo could not see him. There were only two strange wolves. Had something happened to Sim? Throwing caution to the wind, Eevo raced up the slope, with Grosh and Neeth right behind her. The two strange wolves backed off. Suddenly, she saw her brother, lying quietly but seemingly not hurt. He was sound asleep. Eevo stopped as a wave of relief passed over her. She turned and put out both her arms to embrace Neeth and Grosh.

"I see that you two have found yourselves mates," she whispered. "Soon it will be my turn too. But where can I find someone like Dedu or

Seer or Sim? Their kind are hard to find." Now it was her turn to meet the two male wolves that her wolf sisters had brought home.

Eleven

Cubs and More Cubs

The two new members of the pack remained shy, taking some time to become part of cave life. They would enter a cave only if their mates were inside. The only cave they would come into alone was Seer's cave, the Flint Works Cave. But they were afraid of the fire, especially when a fat dripping flare-up occurred. They did, however, lose their fear or shyness with the family, and Grosh's mate seemed to have developed a fondness for Seer, a fondness that was returned. As for the other humans, the two males stayed away from the adults, but tolerated the small children and allowed them to tug and push in play. Sometimes a wolf could even be seen running away, tail between legs, pursued by a toddler barely able to walk. But the response to the older children was different; with them the two newcomers maintained a hands-off policy enforced by intimidating growls.

It was evident that the two females were the dominant animals. It is unusual to have two Alphas of the same sex living together peacefully, but these were sisters who had grown up in the unusual circumstance of total equality. The original cave wolf pack had now grown to four, and soon there was evidence that it was going to grow further. Both Neeth and Grosh were pregnant.

Two moons following their return, the two females began to

indulge in new activities. Eevo noticed that Neeth was spending a good deal of time in the Sun cave. She was rearranging the woodpile at the back of the cave, bringing in some scraps of skins and reeds discarded by Shim. Soon she had created her own private spot.

About three days later, Grosh began similar activity in the Flint Works Cave. She was busy shifting stones to Seer's heap of flints, left in various stages of manufacture and saved fro some future use. Most had not been moved in years. Grosh had chosen a really private place.

Sixty-eight days after her return, Neeth snuck away to her private den. Some hours later, Eevo, who was observing but staying out of the way, was called by Neeth. There they were, four newborn cubs, three female and one male. Groping about, their eyes not open, they somehow found their mother's nipples and attached themselves for feeding. There was a great celebration of wolves and humans.

Four days later Grosh gave birth to her five cubs, two male and three female. This called for another round of celebration. In fourteen days' time, once their eyes were open, the cubs were introduced to the world into which they had been born. It was a wonderful world full of sisters and brothers, parents, uncles and aunts, both four-legged and two-legged. There were wonderful places to explore with things that could be pulled down and dragged about. There were small two-legs to wrestle with and older ones who cuddled, a place of pure heaven.

Seer called a family meeting. He was very pleased with the fact that there were more females than males. "We have to decide how to best deal with the cubs," he announced. "I have long had a dream about a partnership of people with a clever animal. But I never thought that I would see it." He turned to Eevo, "How did you and Sim teach Grosh and Neeth to do all the things that they do? They understand you completely. I almost believe that they know what you are thinking."

She answered simply, "We just lived with them. They were babies so we treated them the way babies are treated. They watched us, played with us and, when we were hunting, even when they were small, they tried to help." She remembered one important point. "Unlike human babies, they grew very quickly. Soon their help was such that almost every hunt was successful."

"Exactly," said Seer. "They also seem to know just what is needed when hunting. In my case, strange as it may seem, Grosh's mate reads all my feelings easily. I may just begin to think of going out of the cave and he will be waiting for me."

"They anticipate everything I want," added Dedu. "Sometimes they know better and are quite ready to correct any mistakes I might

make."

"This," Seer continued, "tells me that wolves are a very clever animal. It's good they seem to like people. They have never attacked us, nor tried to steal our children as hyenas and the big cats do. It seems that wolves and people can form a partnership that will be good for both groups. Now, with the new cubs, we have that chance.

Seer looked very thoughtful. He chose his words carefully before continuing. "We could keep all of them here and just let them grow up as part of the clan. But I think it would be better if we chose a person for each cub. They could live together just as Sim and Eevo did with Neeth and Grosh. It is true that the young need to stay with their mothers until weaned. But the chosen person should be ready to begin to be part of that wolf's life soon after."

"But who can we choose?" asked Eevo. "It would have to be someone who would like them as a brother or sister. Someone who would not become angry when they tear a good skin or steal the meat. There are so many people here. It would be hard for someone to become the main person in one wolf's life."

"Since they were born, I have been thinking about that, Eevo," said Seer. "What do you think of the hunter Ab, Dedu's friend, with his mate Ree? Would they not be a good choice?"

"And Ur and Og," added Sim, "That would be great. But how are they to know?"

Shim spoke up. "It's now the beginning of the pleasant, greening season when all things are beginning to grow. Dedu and I, and perhaps another hunter, could go to the Clan Cave. This is the time of the year that hunters can be spared." Dedu nodded his head, and she continued, "We could invite them to come here and spend two, perhaps three moons getting to know their wolves. They could return for the hunting time with two new hunting helpers." She thought further. "It would let the people of the old clan show how well they can do without the help of their Keepers of the Fire."

Shim turned to Dedu. "We should go soon," she said, "but I suggest that we go by the way I went when I was lost. As a wandering traveller, I remember that the trip took only three and one half days with only one night on the sands. I don't want a long sand crossing again."

"A good idea," said Dedu. "Seer, maybe I could bring back an elk antler or two for you."

"Good," said Seer. "But there are more cubs. I have some friends in the Salt Waters Clan and some in the Good Waters Clan. Maybe they would like to take part. If they are willing to come, we would have started three clan packs beside ours. But each pack should have a male and a female, each from a different litter. Once Neeth and Grosh and their mates get to know the people invited, I don't think they will object. Besides, they already like Ab and Ree, and Ur and Og."

"There is one more cub, preferably a female, that I would like to place," said Eevo. "She should be one of Neeth's puppies. I think she should go to Mee. Her mother is grateful, as are the other mothers, for what the wolves have done. Mee was the one who made the clan realize that wolves can be friends."

"I almost never disagree with you," her brother Sim spoke up quickly, "but I feel that Mee is too young for this. I do think that Mee should be able to play with a young wolf and grow up together with one. But we must remember that wolves grow up faster than people. The wolf will be full-grown long before Mee." He hesitated, then went on. "I think it would be better if the wolf were to live with Seer. Then Mee can come as often as she wishes and play and run with the wolf. That way, the person raising the wolf would be the most reliable and capable person we know. Although he is old in years, he is the most curious and the greatest in knowledge."

"Thank you for those words and feelings, Sim," said Seer. "I am old and had not thought of myself as a suitable person to bring up a young wolf. But as you say, a wolf is full-grown in two years. I may still have that much time. And there are some ideas I have in this experience of wolf and human living together that I would like to try. Little Mee most certainly would provide the exercise a young animal needs. If the others agree, I think that your suggestion is good."

Seer went on to point out other positive points. He noted that the wolves and children were almost inseparable, certainly during the day. At night the wolves would want to roam, but as for safety, the sizeable wolf pack and the experienced hunters would make the Wetlands Clan a safe place for children, probably safer than any other place he could think of. The suggestion that Dedu and Shim be the human partners for the remaining two cubs was accepted. All had been placed.

Seer had described a partnership, but as the wolves had no part in the discussion, or where their homes would be, it really was becoming ownership by the dominant animal. Wolves obey the Alpha animal and Man was assuming that role in the wolf/man relationship.

Hunters were to be sent with messages to Seer's choices in the nearby clans, of Salt Water and the Good Water. Shim and Dedu prepared to leave for the home Cave Clan as soon as it was certain that the passes were clear of snow. They would try to use a route that did not cross the sands.

Since it was now almost the greening season, the weather was pleasant once more and the sun higher in the sky.

Once again, Sim and Eevo would find themselves without parents, but this time in the safety of the Wetlands Clan.

Twelve

A Stranger

Life in the Flint Works Cave was coming along. Working under Seer's instruction, Sim was making very good knives, spear points and scrapers, as well as axes. These were his own design. Now he was concentrating on beauty and not just what weapons could do. His spear shafts were also better. Hunters wanted a spear made by Sim. Each one had excellent balance and a point that was sharp but not so thin that it would break easily. It was a weapon a hunter could trust with his life, a reality for each one of them. They had to know that their weapon would not fail.

Eevo had become a true expert in the art of fire making. At first, people came from neighbouring clans and then, as the news about the Fire Maker spread, they came from far away. These people brought gifts in exchange for knowledge. Sometimes they brought new ideas. All of this increased the wealth of the Wetlands Clan.

One of the earliest arrivals was a young man. His name was Ola and he had come from a very distant clan. His people lived beside a large river, which he described as the mother of all rivers. His people did not live in caves, as there were none. They lived in shelters made of dried bricks of clay, made strong with reeds and woven willow shoots that grew along the riverbank. The river also supplied mud. Every year at the beginning of the greening season, the river would rise and flow over its banks and cover the land for a few days, then go down. Everything left behind was covered in mud. In this mud, grasses grew rapidly and produced seeds that provided food for many birds. In turn, the people ate the birds as well as the seeds. The river also supplied them with many fish. The river, however, although a wonderful source of food, was home to a dreadful predator, an animal called a crocodile. His presence made wading in the river very dangerous.

Flooding had come very early this year, and was much higher than usual. Their Fire Wardens, unprepared for this early flooding, had lost all of their fires. Ola, one of the senior Wardens of the Fire, along with some companions had travelled to the neighbouring clans to get fire. They had to visit a number of clans down river before they could find one where the flooding had not been so great. While making arrangements to get fire, Ola was told of the Fire Maker. A hunter had been told by another hunter from the Salt Water Clan that the Wetlands Clan had a Fire Maker. The story had excited Ola so much that he decided to go to the home of the Fire Maker. A person who taught people how to make fire! Could the story be true? Was it possible for a person to make fire? He had always been taught that it was impossible, but the hunter seemed so sure. If it were so, he could try to learn the secret of fire making. What a discovery that would be! No longer would they have to make long trips to get fire from other people. And besides, fire was so difficult to carry.

After bartering, they acquired the needed fire and his friends returned home with it. Ola, by now determined to find the Fire Maker, decided not to go with them. Instead he got directions to the home of the Wetlands Clan. His decision, however, upset his companions very much. Ola was going without getting permission to do so. Their society was one where people kept strictly to the rules. No one did things independently. Despite their efforts to make Ola change his mind, he refused.

Early the next morning, he set out on a journey that would take almost a full moon of time. Much time was taken walking alongside water that seemed to have no end, water that could not be drunk as it was salty. It was a dangerous trip, and Ola was unarmed since Fire Wardens in his clan do not carry weapons. Often he had no shelter other than to climb a tree at night. Both drinking water and food were hard to find for long stretches of time. This was a journey he really did not want to repeat.

When finally he arrived at the Wetlands Clan, he was exhausted. To his horror, the first to greet him were two huge wolves. They began to force him towards a cave. He tried to turn back, but these wolves were excellent herders. There was no escape. Ola had to head in the direction they wanted him to go. Nearer the cave, a group of small children and young wolves raced toward him, playfully bounding up and down. What was this place where young children and wolves played together? He had never heard of anything like this, but the presence of children made him feel easier. When one little girl turned and called, "Sim," a tall young man wearing a heavy hide apron came out of the cave. Looking up, he could see Ola. When this young man waved his hand, the two wolves sat down nearby. Next, he waved to Ola and signalled him to come to the cave. Although the language being used was different, when coupled with gestures, it became somewhat understandable. Ola noted that the man, or boy, was very tall and walked with a limp.

Sim noticed, as he got closer, that the stranger had a bit of hair growth on his face. The man, although older, was not quite Sim's height, possibly about Eevo's. He looked tired and very scared. Sim could understand the fright as the stranger had been herded by Grosh and her mate. Sim led the way inside the cave.

Taking off his apron and laying it aside, he reached up onto a rock ledge for a packet containing strips of smoked meat, always kept nearby for the evenings he worked late. Sim offered his guest a strip of the meat. Using a gourd, he scooped some water from the chalk water trough. The stranger accepted both and sat down gratefully. He emptied the gourd and looked longingly at the water trough. Sim refilled the gourd, and the stranger drank a little more and started to eat. Suddenly he stopped. Glancing up at Sim, he held up the meat and said slowly his word for "thank you." Sim understood and smiled. The smile was enough for the stranger to relax Sim somewhat. Sim brought out two more pieces of the meat. He put one in front of the man and started eating the other himself. Soon both were talking, gesturing and laughing together, understanding signs if not one another's speech.

The young man, Ola, had never met anyone so openly friendly. Sim's smile and actions made Ola like him at once. This was a wonderful end to a terrible journey. How great it would be if the rumor about the Fire Maker was true! Even though they had not yet exchanged any ideas or thoughts, he felt that he had met a friend. He had so few friends. Their laughter, now being heard in the adjacent caves, soon brought some other people to join them.

An older man and woman and a very much older white-haired man approached. This older man seemed to be the one that the others deferred to with respect. Much to Ola's delight, this man listened to Ola's speech and responded in that language. He greeted Ola, and introduced the others and himself. Ola tried hard to remember their names. They were Sim for the friendly young man, Dedu for the shorter heavy-set man, Shim for his mate who was Sim's mother. The old man's name was Seer. Ola told him his name and that he was a Fire Warden. He had come from the Great River Clan, which lived on the bank of the Great River.

When Seer asked Ola why he had come, Ola told his story about how he had heard of a Fire Maker and why he had decided to find him. He told of how he had journeyed so far and suffered from thirst and from fear that he might not be able to find water. And finally he talked of being surrounded by the wolves and of meeting Sim. Then, turning to Sim, he stated that he had never liked anyone so much on the first meeting. Meeting Sim was like meeting a new-found brother. Seer translated this to Sim who said, "Tell him I feel the same way about him. I thought when I met him, now I have a friend — my first male friend who is not many years older."

Ola next asked about the wolves. Why were people and wolves living together with small children about? He had never imagined anything like it. If there really is a Fire Maker here, he for one would not be surprised.

Seer laughed and explained. "The story of the Fire Maker is true, but the fire maker is not a man, but a woman. There is more than one person in the clan who can make fire, but there is only one Fire Maker who teaches others how to make fire." Ola would be meeting her later. As for the wolves, Seer told him that they were members of the clan. He would learn more about them during his stay at the clan site.

Ola gasped. The Fire Maker a woman? That could not be! It was well-known in his clan that women must not even place wood on a fire. If they touched a fire, it would not burn well. It would go out. If that happened, a special ceremony was required to clean the fire site before it could be used again. Any woman touching fire might even be driven out of the clan. Even men who have not learned the proper ritual were forbidden to touch the sacred fires. Ola noticed Seer looking at him. He hoped that his confusion did not show.

But Seer just smiled and told Ola how the sun itself had taught the Fire Maker the secret of fire and how to release it from wood. He talked of how the Fire Maker had promised the sun that she would teach all who were willing and able to learn.

"Now," Seer said, using the clan language with which Ola was unfamiliar, "Sim, can you take Ola and find a place for him to stay? If you wish, he can stay with you and your family or here in the Flint Works Cave with me. Anywhere you choose. It seems that you like him. It would be good for you to have a friend. By his story, he is one who is as eager to learn as you are. Later you can introduce him to Eevo. He does not yet know that she is your sister and is about his age."

Seer went on to explain, "From the expressions he used, he expects the Fire Maker to be about your mother's age. He is in for a surprise!"

Just then Mee and her friends, both wolf and human, burst into the cave and swarmed everywhere. Then Mee climbed up on Shim's lap and said, "Is he staying? I found him. I think he's nice."

Thirteen

Making Friends

"What a strange clan! But what wonderful togetherness!" Ola thought to himself. Women and even children seemed to have the same rights as men. Even the chief Fire Maker was a woman. The Fire Wardens of his clan would be outraged. It just was not done. But the Fire Maker was not a warden. She was far superior. She could make fire, having been taught by the Sun. All that the Wardens could do was to keep it alight, using all the required ceremonies. What would the official Fire Maker be like? Probably a very strict person, the type of person the Chief Fire Warden of his clan was. There, if anything went wrong, the Fire Warden responsible had to have a good reason for his mistake.

Seer, along with Shim and Dedu, watched as Mee and her companions, always on the move, ran out of the Flint Works Cave for someplace else. Shim turned to Sim and said, "Teach Ola our language so that he won't feel as if everyone is talking about him. That's what it felt like to me when first I came to the clan cave."

"He looks dusty and tired from his travels," thought Sim. "I will take him to the bathing place so he can wash and relax in the water. We can gather some reeds for a bed and make a place for him to sleep in the Flint Works cave. I think I will stay there too." He signalled Ola to come with him. The two young men walked away, one with a noticeable limp.

"Those two will be good for each other," said Dedu. "Sim has never had a friend close to his age. Remember when he was very small? The others about his age would have nothing to do with him. They just made fun of his lameness. Our people even tossed him out of the cave when we left for here."

"I don't think Ola has had much of a boyhood either," Seer replied. "The clan he comes from is a larger group than most, about as big as ours. But it doesn't allow much freedom for the children while they are growing up. It's a very organized group, not like the family group that we have here."

Seer went on to describe Ola's clan. "The clan Ola comes from is made up of a number of groups. The Fire Wardens come from the original clan of people. They make the decisions for the whole group, and only the very brightest of the wardens are allowed into their council. The lower-ranking people are mostly the hunters. They obey their leader, much like a very large wolf pack."

Seer hesitated and thought more about Ola. "But he is different. He chose to leave to find the Fire Maker. That shows that he can think and act on his own. But it also means that he would be considered a trouble-maker." Seer warned of a possible danger. "If Ola goes back without having found what he left for, he will likely be punished for leaving without permission. Even if he goes back with something of value he could still be in trouble. He would be closely watched all the time." That group, as Seer remembered them, liked order in all things and discouraged creativity. He shook his head. "That is what happens when clans get too big. Did you notice? While we were talking together, he was watching us closely to see who was in charge. He could not decide. For Ola, that is confusing. Having someone like Sim with him will be good."

"They will be good for each other," remarked Shim. "But we must prepare for our trip back to get Ab and Og and either Ur or Ree. I hope both come."

Sim and Ola, accompanied by the wolves, left the cave sites and walked toward the bathing spot area by the river. Sim removed his body covering and suggested by sign language that Ola do the same. He ran and jumped into the water. Ola hesitated and looked fearful, glancing along the riverbanks as though expecting something frightening.

Sim noticed Ola's reluctance. "He acts just the way Ab did when he heard the crashing in the bush that time the wolves drove the elk toward us. There must be something in the water where he lives that he fears," he thought to himself. Getting out of the water, he went up to Ola.

With gestures and occasional words, Sim asked what he feared. Ola understood. By pantomime he described a large animal that lived in the river at his home. It was a powerful predator. Sim could not believe that it could be nearly as big as described. "Not here," said Sim. "There's only some fish and a few small animals." Somewhat reassured, Ola slowly made his way into the water. Soon he was relaxing in the soothing liquid.

A short while later, as they started back, Ola could hear someone coming towards them. The two wolves bounded forward eagerly. He could hear laughter and, as they turned at a bend in the path, he could see a very pretty, tall young woman playing with them. She came toward them.

She was more than pretty. She was beautiful and somewhat familiar looking. Then it struck him. She looked a lot like the older woman they had called Shim and like his new-found companion Sim. When she came closer, Sim introduced her as Eevo. Ola told her his name and she repeated it, "Ola." There was something in the way she said it that made Ola feel odd in a very pleasant way.

Since Eevo had been on her way to bathe, Sim and Ola and the wolves returned to the river with her. Sim told her what he knew about Ola and that he had come from very far away to learn how to make fire. Eevo told Sim that she hoped that Ola would be better than the woman she had been teaching these days. Ola, trying to make out what was being said as they tried to keep him in the conversation, got the idea that Eevo worked in the Fire Maker's cave and had been given a bad time. He decided that he did not like the Fire Maker. He knew he could not like anyone who could make Eevo unhappy.

After bathing, splashing and laughing together, the three young people returned to the caves. "This was fun," said Sim, "It's like being with Ree and Ur again."

"Better," said Eevo.

They returned to the Flint Works Cave and set up a sleeping place for Ola. As he lay down to have his first sleep free from danger, Eevo and Sim talked for a while. Eevo suggested that they wait for a few days to let Ola become acquainted with the Wetlands area. It would be better if he could learn at least some of the clan language before coming to the Cave of the Sun. This would help her give him instruction in fire making. It was obvious that he was experienced in looking after fires. She said to Sim, "I like him. I hope it takes him a long time to learn."

"I like him too," Sim replied. "Perhaps he will like it so much here that he will want to stay."

"That would be very good," agreed Eevo.

The next morning, they said goodbye to Shim and Dedu. And for the next few days they were busy with language lessons, learning about clan customs and doing some general exploration of the area all around the clan lands. Since the language was fairly simple, with a relatively small vocabulary, while they were teaching Ola the language of the Wetlands Clan language, they learned his. By using gestures and expressions to help give much of the meaning to words, Ola could speak to the people about him within a week.

Seer helped a great deal since he knew Ola's language. Seer was especially amused when he realized that Ola was still not aware that Eevo was the Fire Maker, a person whom Ola had somehow come to dislike and fear. And so, Ola was in no hurry to start fire-making lessons. One evening, as the three young people were talking, Eevo brought the matter up. "Sim, tomorrow will you bring Ola up to the Sun Cave about mid-morning? I will be busy until then."

Ola grimaced. "I don't think I am going to like this very much," he confided. "I have a thought picture of the Fire Maker as a fierce old woman. She will make fun of me if I make any errors."

"Absolutely right," said Sim with a straight face. "They don't come any nastier."

Eevo started to laugh. "Who gave you that description?"

"No one. It's just an impression I made knowing what the Chief Fire Warden is like."

"Despite what Sim says, I think you may be pleasantly surprised when you meet her tomorrow," said Eevo.

Ola did not look convinced. Sim, taking pity on him, said. "Ola, forgive us for laughing but you will be pleasantly surprised. You are now sitting and talking to the two fire makers in this or any clan. Eevo was the one who discovered how to release fire from wood, and she is the one they call the Fire Maker."

Ola looked startled.

"No, don't get up, and stop looking frightened," Sim tried to reassure him. "I will tell you how it all came about. You speak our language well enough now so you can be told the story. Both Eevo and I like you. You seem like one of us, even if you come from another clan."

After Eevo and Sim told their story, Ola was amazed. "All this happened two years ago when you were still small children. Especially you, Sim, you say that you grew to almost the size you are now in that one year. Your friend Ab might very well be right in saying that you have been chosen by the Sun. I wonder what the wise men of my home would say?" All three sat and talked well into the night. Their friendship became even closer

Fourteen

A Challenge

Ola admired the beautifully shaped, extremely sharp weapons that Sim and Seer made. He had never seen anything like them. Sim was surprised, "I thought that your people had spears. Seer said that yours is a very advanced society."

"It is," said Ola, "but we have none of this hard stone you use. We use bone, shaped and sharpened for many uses. Our spears are good for spearing fish. And my people eat a lot of fish. But bone is useless against the heavy scaly plates that cover the terrible animal I told you about — the one we call Crocodile. Those monsters kill many of my people. The sabre-toothed tiger you described sounds just as dangerous. But you can't attack a crocodile the same way. I'm not sure that even your best spear would be able to make a dent in the scales of the crocodile."

"Just how big is this animal? How thick is its skin? You say scales. Is it a fish that can walk on land?" asked Sim.

Ola tried to describe the crocodile. "It is as long as three or four men, end to end. Some are larger. It is as thick and wide as three men, two lying side-by-side, with a third man on top. Its skin is about as thick as a man's hand from front to back. The skin has overlapping, hard thick plates that break our bone spears. The beast has four rather short legs, but it can run as quickly as the fastest land animal."

Ola talked about the powerful, long tail of the crocodile. He said that one blow from the tail could break a man's back. He described its mouth as being the length of a large man's arm, with long sharp gripping teeth that grab its prey and do not let go. Ola admitted that his people had never killed an adult one but had found some dead. Occasionally when coming across a young one, they had succeeded in killing it. But even that was difficult. They, too, are quite dangerous. Ola went on to talk about the crocodiles spending most of their time either in the water with only their nostrils and eyes showing or lying on the mud bank of the river. There, they look much like a log of a tree deposited there by the river. "They may look harmless, but that is only a camouflage. Crocodiles are always ready to attack anything that approaches."

Sim listened with amazement. "Nothing scares them?"

"Almost nothing. The water mammoth is about the only animal they avoid. When annoyed, that huge beast had been known to kill one of them," Ola replied.

"You describe a terrible animal. The wolves wouldn't be useful in a fight with something like that," Sim said, trying to imagine such an enemy. "But weapons of the right sort might well be. When Dedu and the others come, we will tell them about this crocodile. They might have suggestions. Tell me, how do these crocodiles attack?"

"On land they charge with their jaws open to grab the animal they're after. Then they drag their catch into the water and pull it under, until it dies. What they do after that I don't know." Ola paused, trying to remember. "In the water they just pull the victim down. Even animals as large and strong as the lion may be attacked."

"If they attack with open mouths, then their scales won't protect them," observed Sim. "Two, or better still, three sharp heavy-shafted spears thrust into their throats should make them act as the tiger did with one oil-soaked burning spear in its mouth." Sim began to like the challenge. "Your crocodile is beginning to interest me. A hunt of that kind would really test the weapons I make."

Sim began to describe a new type of spear, one with a heavier shaft, one that would not break when it came into contact with a moving heavy creature like a crocodile. "Yes," he said, "I'm going to try to make one."

"You will just go ahead and make something like that? Don't you have to ask for permission first from the clan's elders?" Ola was astonished.

"Oh, I will speak to Seer while you are with Eevo in the Cave of the Sun, but why would I ask permission? This is something I choose to do, and so I do it. How else does someone go about doing the things they know how to do?" This time Sim was surprised.

"The longer I stay here the more differences I see between life in this clan and mine. We have to have approval for anything we do. No one would ever think of doing something without permission. That would bring some type of punishment," replied Ola.

"Did you get approval to find the Fire Maker?" asked Sim. "It seems to me that you did so despite your companions' opposition."

"Quite true," said Ola, thinking back on his decision to strike out on his own. "And I don't know what gave me the courage. Once done, there was no going back. I'm very worried about what will happen to me when I go back. Maybe if I bring back the secret of fire making, I will escape the worst. But they will keep a close eye on me!"

"Why go back?" asked Sim. "You could stay here. Eevo and I would like that. I'm sure that Seer would be pleased and the others of the clan would approve."

"I am a Fire Warden and I came to find how to make fire. Once I learn how, if I do, I must go back to teach my people the secret. It is my duty. I gave a promise to care for the fires of my clan and I must do so. Once I go back, there is no way that I would be allowed to return here." Ola looked sad. "If only I could go home, give them the secret, then return to Eevo and you. But that's only a dream."

Sim looked at Ola. "It may be possible," he said. "For now, learn how to make fire, and I know that you will. But don't be in a hurry to go back to your home. The others coming here with Father and Mother will be able to help. Together, we may be able to solve your problem."

"But how?" asked Ola.

"Give me a little time to do some thinking. I'll talk with Seer," said Sim. "Your dream may soon be more than a dream. Now the sun is high and Eevo will be waiting. I'll walk up to the Cave of the Sun with you."

Fifteen

From Fire to Plans

Eevo was waiting for them in the upper cave that had been set aside for the teaching of fire making. The opening of the cave faced the position where the sun came up at the time of the moons when both day and night were about equal in length. This was the time of the beginning of the greening season and the beginning of the falling leaf time.

Ola looked around. Neat stacks of dry wood, about the length of a person's forearm, and about half the thickness, were against one wall. There were bundles of smaller pieces of wood that had been pounded with rock hammers so that the wood was all splintered. As well, there were bunches of dried crushed leaves and some fine pieces of dry bark, the tinder for starting the first flame. Stacked against another wall were flat boards also about the length of a person's a forearm and the width of a hand. All were about the thickness of a finger. Along with these boards were a similar number of small wooden rods of the same length, and as thick around as a man's thumb. At first Ola thought that they were small saplings. But when Eevo handed him one of the sticks and a board, he saw that they were really pieces of wood. They had been carefully shaped so that they were straight and somewhat rounded.

Eevo understood that Ola was quite experienced in looking after fires. "You know what size of wood is best suited for the various stages of fire lighting. I don't need to show you that. Let's start. I always thank the Sun before attempting to light a new fire. I know how lucky I was at my first attempt. Had I used wood other than the kind I did, or of a different size, I now know that I wouldn't have succeeded. The Sun must have guided me. Ab says that it is the Sun that makes all life possible. So I ask all the people I teach to thank the Sun in their own way before they try to make fire." Eevo went to the entrance of the cave and raised both arms in a salute to the Sun.

"Now we're ready." Eevo placed one of the flat boards down on the cave floor, and knelt down in front of it. She picked up the shaped wooden rod and placed its gently rounded tip against a slight depression that had been made near one edge of the board. She changed her grip so that the wooden rod was between her palms, and proceeded to spin the rod as rapidly as she could. At the same time, she applied pressure against the board. Soon a bit of greyish powder was ground off the rod and the board. Eevo continued, concentrating on her work. The powder became darker in colour and a wisp of smoke appeared. Suddenly, a reddish glow came from the powder which had gathered where the spinning rod and the board met. Eevo fanned the tiny glowing ember with her hand, then tilted the board so that the ember dropped into a prepared bed of the crushed leaves, dry bark and splintered wood. Gently she blew on it. A small flame appeared. Eevo then picked up another handful of the prepared tinder and put it down beside the board. Handing the rod to Ola, she said, "Now, you try it."

Picking up the spinning rod and examining it, Ola felt and smelled the end that had been applied to the board. It was charred. He scraped it against the stone floor of the cave to remove the burned portion. He then looked at the flat board and, borrowing Sim's flint knife, made a fresh pit about a thumb's width away from the previously-used depression, now somewhat burned from the previous firemaking. He did not fail to notice the look of satisfaction on both Eevo's and Sim's face. Next he practised making the fire rod spin between his palms. Once satisfied, he turned his attention to the tinder and made sure that it was really dry and close by. He also checked to make certain that a number of small dry pieces of wood were within reach. He was ready.

Squatting on the cave floor, he placed the fire board directly in front of himself, then put the freshly-scraped point of the fire rod into the cavity he had made. Ola began to rotate the rod, slowly increasing the speed of the spinning. Once he stopped and gently touched the working end of the fire rod. He winced, "Good, it's hot." He started the rod spinning in its groove again. Soon he was rewarded with a small collection of powder. As this darkened, it started to smoke. Then came the hoped-for ember. This he transferred to his tinder and gently blew it into a flame. Carefully, he added the small pieces of wood. As they caught fire, some larger ones were put in place. In a very short time he had a good well-laid fire burning.

"Well done, Ola," said Sim. "You are only the second person to get a fire started the first time. You and Eevo. I had to try a number of times before I could."

"Yes, very well done," said Eevo. "Now you must learn which trees provide wood that makes good fire-boards and good rods. I will show you. You're quick. None of the ones I have taught mastered the art in fewer than four days."

It was then that Sim told Eevo the bad news. Soon Ola would have to return to his own people to show them the secret of fire making. He might not be allowed to return. Eevo's face fell.

"But maybe not all is bad," said Sim. "I have a plan that might let Ola come back to the Wetlands Clan. It will depend on what Dedu and Mother think. But I want to discuss it with you two and Seer first."

Leaving the Cave of the Sun, the three started down the hillside towards the Flint Works Cave. Seer saw them coming. Something in the way they walked caused him some concern. What could be wrong?

"Was there some problem?" he asked.

"Oh, no, Ola started a fire on his very first attempt. He is as good as we are," said Eevo. "But we need to talk with you. As a Fire Warden, Ola feels that he must return to his people now that he can make fire. It's his duty and responsibility. We understand that, but Ola fears that he will not be allowed to return here. Sim has an idea which he thinks might work. He wants to talk with all of us. We've come down to eat and talk," said Eevo.

"Very well. Let's do so. Who's starting?" Seer welcomed the opportunity.

Both Eevo and Ola were looking at Sim. He hesitated, then began, "This morning I was working on a large spearhead that I was making for Ab to hunt large animals like the elk. Ola came in. When he saw the spearhead, he wondered if a spear like that could penetrate the thick plates of the fierce animal that lives in the great river at his home. I did not know that Ola's people didn't have sharp flint tools. Their hunters use sharpened bone tools, useless against this huge and very dangerous crocodile." Seer nodded. He, too, had heard of the crocodile. Indeed, it was dangerous. He asked Sim to continue. "When Ola described the animal's way of attacking, I began to feel that with well-designed weapons in the hands of good hunters, the animal could be stopped. It was just a thought in my head."

Sim talked about Ola's fear that the leaders of his clan would keep him from leaving once he returned. While this had seemed strange to Sim, he understood Ola's sense of duty. But he felt that Ola should be able to come back when he wanted to.

Then an idea had taken shape in Sim's mind. He described it. "We have young wolves to train in hunting and in understanding our signals. This is best done away from the clan lands. Our experience with Neeth and Grosh has taught us that it takes about three or four moons to accomplish this. Also, I have new weapons I would like to try against the crocodile. To hunt so strong an animal requires very good hunters. We need hunters who have worked together and know each other's signals. They must have trust in each other. Such a group of hunters will be here in a few days. This means we could have well-armed people and twelve wolves, four adult ones and eight rapidly growing ones, going with Ola. I believe that together we can kill one of the crocodiles which all of Ola's people fear. If we do, I feel that there would be no opposition to Ola coming back with us. But only after he and Eevo teach the people how to make fire."

Ola sat open-mouthed. Eevo just smiled.

Seer laughed. "Sim, are you a tool maker? A hunter? Or are you clever in making people do what you want? That scheme might work. There's no threat made. But the leaders of Ola's clan wouldn't fail to note that, if they refused Ola permission to go, they might be in danger. They wouldn't want to take on a band of armed hunters with wolves, not at all! They would let Ola go. And yes, Sim, if Ola returned alone, they would honour him for bringing back the ability to make fire. But they would make sure that they controlled the secret. Ola might even be in danger after they had learned how to make fire. Remember, Ola has shown that he will think on his own. What if he passed on the secret to the people? That would mean that the Wardens would lose their power."

Seer thought some more about the idea. The three waited. Finally, he said, "Sim, your scheme is probably the best way. But do you really think that you can conquer the great crocodile? I have seen them. No one has ever, as I understand, killed an adult one."

Sim did not feel discouraged. "If they attack as Ola describes, we won't have to do much. They will do it for us. Our heavy flint spears are the secret. I must get busy and make at least two spears for each hunter." He felt really confident. "After the hunt, when we come back, we can leave some spears for the hunters of Ola's clan. They can free themselves from a terrible predator."

Seer just laughed again. "I see that you have already completed the trip and hunt."

Ola looked at the others in amazement. "You would do this for me? But, Sim, you have never seen the crocodile. You don't know how terrible an animal it is."

"Ola, you have never seen Dedu and Mother on a hunt, nor Ab or Og. And don't forget the wolves," said Eevo.

"And, of course, you two," reminded Seer. "I remember the hyena fight."

He then told Ola of the hyena attack on the clan infants and how, in the time it takes to take thirty breathes, nine hyenas were dead and five running away. "But we must wait for the others before we plan the actual hunt," he cautioned. "None of them have ever seen this crocodile. It's very powerful. They'll want to find out all you know about it and its habits. This way they can plan to remove as much danger as possible."

"Remove the danger? That's impossible. No one has ever hunted the crocodile. Everyone is too fearful of its strength and speed. Seer, you talk of a hunt like this as if it were just an ordinary hunt," Ola replied. He could not believe what he was hearing.

"All hunts must be planned. Good hunters think carefully about the risks and study the animal they hunt. All hunts have some danger, so it is the duty of the hunter to make the dangers as small as possible. People are not the fastest or strongest animal, but people plan and think. In turn, they are seldom hunted but are almost always the hunters," Seer explained
.   He returned his attention to Sim. "Now, Sim, let's start making more of the large spearheads. If the others agree, we will have the equipment for this hunt. But what about your foot? This will be a long trip."

"As I get older and stronger I seldom think of it at all," answered Sim. "Anyway, right now, I must work on the weapons we will need."

With that, the two flint knappers left the cave. Ola watched them go, still flabbergasted at the speed with which the plans were being made.

Sixteen

Hunting Horses

The chief hunter, the leader while Dedu was away, reported that a herd of horses had been seen. He wanted to organize a hunt. Would Sim or Eevo help? They were the ones the wolves would follow. Eevo said that she would since Sim was busy making larger spearheads. A hunt would be good. They would need dried smoked meat and more water bags for the trip back to Ola's clan. There were few water sources along the route that Ola had taken. With so many people going, they would need a good supply of water. Besides, this would give her a chance to introduce Ola to hunting with the help of the wolves.

"Have you been on a hunt for large animals?" Eevo asked Ola.

"I have never been on any hunt," said Ola. "I have always been a Fire Warden. I was taught to only look after the duties of fire care, nothing else. How much better your way is! You and Sim do anything you want. You never need permission to do something new. But would the hunters allow me to go? Wouldn't I spoil things?"

"Of course you can come. No, you won't spoil things. You and I will go with Neeth and her mate at first light tomorrow. Grosh can look after the cubs. Our role is to locate the herd and start the horses moving toward the other hunters. But you need to know how to use a spear. I'll show you. I like light spears with a long narrow blade. They suit me best."

Off they went towards Seer's cave, Eevo still talking. "Come, I'll pick up two spears for each of us. We'll need some fire-hardened ones to practice throwing. Don't worry, we'll do our practising where no one can watch us."

The two picked up the spears they wanted and left. Seer looked at Sim and said, "I would very much like to keep that young man in our clan."

"So would I," agreed Sim.

The following morning, as soon as there was a hint of light in the sky, Eevo, Neeth and her mate came to the Flint Works Cave. There was Ola, up and waiting.

"He's been up much of the night," Sim said. "Take him away so I can get some sleep." And he rolled over, pulled his fur up over his head and went back to sleep.

"I've brought some dried meat. We can eat as we travel," said Eevo, as they started toward the grassland where the herd had been seen.

"I'm nervous," said Ola. "I don't know what I'm doing. I just know I'll spoil the hunt. Are you sure I should come?"

"Of course I'm sure! There's no way that you will upset anything. The wolves will do most of the work. Remember the plan." Eevo went back over the hunt plan. The main hunting party was now gathering at the shallow river crossing, downstream from the caves. They would hide there and wait. Eevo and Ola and the two wolves were to swing around the area where the horses were. Once the herd was between them and the river, they were to begin the drive.

Eevo kept walking and talking to Ola. "If the wind continues to blow in the direction it is now, by the time that we are in the right position, our scent will be getting to the horses. They'll begin to get nervous. It's then we'll try to be noisy. The herd will start to run away from us. That's when the wolves will play their role. They'll keep the herd moving toward the river and keep it from moving either to the left or right. Once the horses see their familiar river crossing, they will run toward it to escape from us. Right there is where the hunters will spring out of hiding to get as many as they can. You see, our part of the hunt is easy."

Ola listened to all this and said little. He was having some difficulty keeping up with Eevo and the two wolves. But he could not bring himself to ask for a slower pace. By now the sun was just beginning to show a line of bright light above the distant hills. They had been downwind from the horse herd and the wolves had caught the scent of the hunt. Now their little group swung in a circle until the horses were now downwind from them, and near enough to be seen. The stallions were tossing their heads sensing some danger. Only one avenue seemed a safe escape. The herd took it.

The hunt took on new meaning for Ola. He was so excited that his fatigue was gone. He and Eevo were running together behind the herd. The wolves on either flank kept the herd moving in the direction Eevo wanted. As soon as the horses began to smell the water, herding was no longer necessary. They were racing to the water crossing. Eevo called to Ola, who by now was almost winded. She pointed out a young stallion and began to edge closer to it. With one spear ready in her hand, she put on a burst of speed and ran alongside. Ola saw her bring her arm back and then thrust it ahead. The spear entered the animal's chest just behind the lower ribs, causing it to stumble and then fall. Eevo's second spear made sure that it was a clean kill.

The horse herd with the two wolves as flankers continued their run for the river crossing unaware of the hunters who waited there. Ola came up to Eevo and collapsed. He sat on the ground taking huge gasps of air. It took a few moments before he could talk. His first words were, "After seeing you in action, I'm not so sure the crocodile will win!"

Seventeen

A Chance Discovery

Eevo felt proud. It had been a very successful hunt. There would be plenty of meat since six more horses had been killed by the clan hunters at the river crossing. All the next day the clan was busy skinning and cutting up the meat. The fresh liver, always the reward of the hunter who had killed the animal, was in sufficient supply so that all members of the clan could share. The wolves, as usual, claimed the entrails and the kidneys. But each stomach and bladder, along with a large sac-like portion of gut, the caecum, that is especially large in horses, was handled with care. These were to be preserved by smoke to be used as more water bags. This was Eevo's job.

There was a huge amount of meat to be smoked and dried and another huge amount to be roasted for the feast that followed every successful hunt. Because the Flint Works cave was furthest from the living quarters and closest to the river where the meat had been cut up, its fire was used for the roasting and smoking of meat. By the end of the day, much fat had dripped into the ashes of the fire. Everyone was tired, and no one wanted to clean up. A very tired and dirty threesome, Ola and Eevo and Sim, went to the bathing place to soak in the water that had been warmed by the afternoon sun.

"Did you enjoy your first hunt?" asked Sim.

"Very much," said Ola, "but I will have to learn to run if I hope to keep up with Eevo, let alone the wolves."

Sim laughed, "So you experienced Eevo's running? Only one person I know can keep up with her. That is our mother, Shim. So don't feel bad."

"He did well," said Eevo. "He kept pace with the horses and very few hunters can do that."

"There is no way that I had the strength to even raise a spear. Yet she thrust her spear into the horse's side, exactly where she wanted it, while running. She acted as if she was on the practice field, not at all like someone who had been running all morning," said Ola.

"You did well, Ola," repeated Sim. "When we have a boastful hunter, Dedu arranges that he is placed between Mother and Eevo on the next hunt that requires running. Somehow that always stops the boasting."

About noon the next day, Neeth and Grosh became bouncy, acting almost like cubs. They ran off toward the hills. Very shortly, the two wolves and five people could be seen — Mother, Dedu, Ab and Ro, but only one woman. As they came closer, Eevo could see that it was Ree. Why had Ur not come? Eevo and Sim, with help from Ola, prepared food for their arrival.

The travellers were first welcomed and then subjected to a barrage of questions, everyone speaking at once. For the first time since coming to the Wetlands Clan, Ola felt like a stranger. He stayed back, but not for long. Sim spotted him and literally pulled him into the group. Seer, laughing with pleasure at all this exuberance, finally was able to make himself heard and suggested that all sit down and eat. Then the story of their trip could be told. The smell of fresh, roasting horse meat reminded the travellers of their hunger and a general feasting began.

The question as to why Ur had not come was answered by Mother. The people of the Cave Clan were still a little fearful of the fire. As yet, none had succeeded in lighting a fire. That was one reason. The second was better. Ur was in the middle part of her first pregnancy. A period of prolonged travel, in Shim's opinion, especially as it was not necessary, was not wise. So although they missed her, Sim and Eevo were glad she had not come, especially considering what they hoped to do. Yes, they had used the route that Mother remembered from the time she first got lost. It had required considerable more climbing, but had shortened the trip by almost two days each way.

Ree and Ab and Og were introduced to the two cubs they would be responsible for teaching as soon as they were weaned. They intended to be the constant companions of the cubs. In the late afternoon, accompanied by Grosh, they set out on a "get to know one another" excursion and returned before sunset.

This was to be the routine. It had been worked out by Sim and Eevo to match, as much as possible, their experience with Neeth and Grosh when they were cubs. There were, however, two differences. Each pair of cubs were not siblings and each pair was made up of a male and a female except for Dedu and Shim's pair, who were female. Once the others from the Good Water and Salt Water clans arrived, the training exercise was to be for longer periods, with no returns to the Wetlands caves for three or four days at a time. Different territory was to be covered by each group during the training session. The original plan had called for four moons of training, which would still leave plenty of time for the various groups to return to their home caves before the cold weather set in. Now Sim, Eevo and Seer were planning to change this but had not as yet told the others of their plans. That would have to wait until each group had learned the cooperation and complete trust required between the wolf cubs and their humans.

The next day saw the arrival of the hunter from the Good Water clan, a man named Sill. Two days later, the Salt Water Clan hunter, called Grew, and the messenger Seer had sent arrived. Both men from the other clans knew each other well and were good friends of Seer's. They were mature hunters, about as old as Dedu and of about equal experience. The whole affair got off to a good start, with the people involved with the training of hunters and wolves finding that they liked each other. It was Mee who introduced Grew to Neeth and Grosh and also to Mine, her name for the wolf cub Seer imagined was his pupil. Mee knew better.

Over the next few days, because of all this activity, no one had cleaned up the increasingly smelly mess made by the ashes and the fat from the roasting fire. Since by now the fear of predators had almost disappeared in the Wetlands Clan and, with fire now so easy to get, that particular fire had been allowed to go out. The wandering twosome of Mee and Mine came on the stinking mess of ashes and fat. As there had been a number of warm days, this mixture smelled even worse than hyenas. The cub thought that this was a perfect thing to roll in and, of course, Mee did what the cub did. The two very proud and amazingly smelly individuals returned to the Flint Works cave, proud of their new odour. Seer, who was making a spear shaft, got a whiff and almost gagged. Quickly he shooed them out of the cave, toward the bathing place. Shim, hearing the "Out! out!" stepped out of her cave and saw Seer driving the two along. She too picked a bit of their horrible aroma.

"What did they do to smell so bad?" she asked Seer.

"I don't know. They must have been dead for a moon to smell like that," he answered with a grin. "We will probably have to bury them, or at least put them into the river to soak."

Mee looked startled. "Don't do that!" she cried. "All we did was play in the ashes."

"Well, I vote for a soak in the water," insisted Shim. "I don't think either has ever been at the bathing place. I'll get in the water too to make sure that Mee scrubs well with sand and I will wash the cub."

"With my help," offered Seer. "Cubs can be rather squirmy."

At the bathing place all four got into the water. The cub liked it. Mee, interested in finding it to be all right, felt that she should complain anyway and began to squirm. Shim, in trying to hold onto this slippery girl, happened to push her under the water. A sputtering Mee came up and began to rub her eyes and face. She shook her head. Surprisingly, foamy suds began to cover her hair and face. The more she rubbed, the more the suds appeared. Shim was now very interested. Seer had begun to rub the cub's coat and was rewarded with a mass of sudsy bubbles. "Shim, "he called, "this mixture of fat and ashes has made something new. Whatever it is, it does clean things. The bad smell even disappears in water."

"Amazing!" exclaimed Shim. "I've have never seen a child as clean as it is making Mee."

"It's burning my eyes. I want to get out," complained Mee.

"Rinse your eyes with water," said Shim. "Where did you get this stuff?"

"From where the fire was. Where the horse meat was roasted," Mee replied. "I'll never go there again, ever! I don't like water." Just then the cub, now clean, went paddling by. Mee, forgetting how much she hated water, rediscovered how much fun splashing could be.

Shim turned to Seer, "I believe those two have discovered something very useful. I'll get some and try it on myself."

"Bring enough for me too," said Seer. "It seems to work far better than scrubbing sand. It's not as rough on skin."

Eevo, Sim and Ola, arriving a little later, just stood there and stared. Shim, her hair covered with white bubbles running down her back and chest, was rubbing something on Seer's back. Seer's beard and hair had never looked whiter.

"Come in and try some," coaxed Shim. "This cleans far better than sand and is pleasant. It smells horrid but, mixed with water, it loses most of that awful smell."

"What is it?" asked Eevo.

"A mixture of fat and ash," replied Seer. "It seems that mixing the two creates something new."

He then lowered himself into the water, rinsed and came out of the pool. Shim also rinsed herself and, pointing to a slimy substance in a chalk container, said, "Try it."

The others looked at one another, then shrugged. They removed their light animal skin coverings and stepped into the pond. Soon there was a flurry of soap suds, followed by squeals of pleasure.

"There must be some way to get rid of that smell," said Sim. "I will try ashes from different types of wood." Splashes from both Eevo and Ola silenced him.

"How like him!" said both Shim and Seer together as they burst out in laughter.

Eighteen

To The Great River

About ten days after the arrival of the Salt Water Clan hunter, Sim and Eevo felt that the group was ready for the next stage. The humans and wolves had lived together, slept and eaten together. Strong relationships had been formed. Now was the time to tell them of the possible expedition, the reason for it and for the hunt of that most dangerous of predators, the crocodile. Seer took the lead in presenting the story. He told of how and why Ola had come. He told the others of how Ola's clan worked and how, if Ola went back alone, he could never return to the Wetlands Clan, where he was wanted. It was Ola's strong sense of duty that was forcing him to return. He felt that he must give his people the secret of fire making. But it was possible that Ola would be in danger.

   Ola's people lived in the area that the crocodile inhabited. The weapons his people had were useless against the hard plates that covered the animal's body. But Sim had developed spearheads he believed would penetrate this tough covering. Originally, these spearheads were made to be used against very big animals. Now, here was a dangerous animal that had, over the years, killed and eaten a large number of the people from Ola's clan. This animal was never hunted because it was so large and dangerous. People believed it was impossible to kill an adult crocodile. From what Ola had said about it, it was not a clever animal. But Sim was sure that since it had never been hunted, it shouldn't be too hard to confuse when under attack.

A trip to Ola's clan was a long journey, through all types of country. It would be an ideal training opportunity for the wolf cubs as there would not be so many people around to distract the cubs. And it would be a good way to try out all of Sim's new weapons.

The plan was to have a strong party of well-armed hunters, accompanied by the woman who had received the gift of making fire from the Sun itself, appear at the clan's home area. They were to be brought to Ola's clan by Ola, in order to teach the making of fire. If this group of hunters also killed the animal that could not be killed, Ola's clan would be impressed. After teaching the Fire Wardens how to make fire, they would ask that Ola return with them to the Wetlands Clan. Seer felt that there would be no objections from the elders of Ola's clan. This was to be a friendly excursion to test new weapons and to give more people the great gift of fire making. No one would be threatened. Once he finished his talk, Seer turned the meeting over to the hunters to discuss.

Dedu jokingly asked, "Could Sim have something to do with this?"

After some thought Dedu added, "If Sim has thought it out, it will be possible. But first we must learn all we can about this animal. I assume that the only one who has seen one is Ola. Is that right?"

"No, I have seen one," said Seer. "But let Ola describe it."

All nodded. Ola began saying that he had seen a crocodile on a number of occasions, but not up close.

"Then describe it to us as closely as you can," said Dedu. "What does it look like? How fast can it move? How does it hunt? Is it solitary, like the sabre-toothed tiger, or does it travel in packs like hyenas?"

"What do they look like?" repeated Ola. "Well, the closest I can get is very much like a gecko, those little lizards that we so often see chasing insects, only much bigger. How fast do they move? Well, you know how fast a gecko can move. How does it hunt? Again like the gecko, it stays absolutely still until its prey is in position and then it charges." He looked at Dedu. "Until you asked those specific questions, I had not thought of the similarity between the crocodile and the little gecko."

"When you describe it in that way, somehow your terrible crocodile becomes far less terrible," said Grew, the hunter from the Salt Water Clan.

"If you think of yourself as a beetle and the gecko as a gecko, it becomes terrible again." Ola continued, "A large one can be as long as four men and as wide as three. As to speed, maybe Eevo could outrun it but I couldn't."

"It's that big and that fast!" exclaimed Dedu.

Ola went on to describe the heavy protective scales or plates that covered the crocodile's body, the great mobile tail that was a deadly weapon to be avoided, and its habit of pulling its prey into the water and drowning its catch. He described the way the crocodile charged, opening its mouth to grab its prey. He said that smaller ones congregated together with others of like size but stayed well away from the big ones that might eat them. The large ones were very territorial. Each would not tolerate another in its area. The little gecko suddenly became a crocodile. It was beginning to sound as if it would be impossible for people to beat it.

Seer, however, reminded them that people could think, but crocodiles could not. Sim had devised weapons he thought would work. Never having been attacked, it had no defense against a well-thought-out attack. Sim continued the idea of the plan by describing the weapons he had made. The large spearheads were mounted on extra-strong shafts, long enough so that they could be braced against the ground. He felt these spear shafts could withstand the weight of the crocodile's charge. Sim said that with the way the crocodile charged, with its mouth open, it could very well impale itself on the spear and make the hunt easy. Furthermore, he said that the large animal's territorial instincts meant that there would not be another one around to attack the hunters.

Sim then showed them the special weapon he had made. It was a two-headed, very short spear, unlike anything seen before. The shaft was as long and as thick as a man's forearm from the elbow to the wrist. On each end was a large spearhead firmly attached with the broad flint base overlapping the shaft so that once it penetrated it would not pull out. A long rawhide cord was tied firmly to the shaft below one of the spear-heads. Sim produced a long spear shaft. One end was notched ready for a spearhead. The portion below the notch was bound in rawhide but there was no spearhead. Sim forced the notch over the middle of his very short two-headed spear.

"This is what we will use to thrust into the crocodile's mouth," he explained. "I expect, or rather hope, that it will bite down on it, and drive one or, with luck, both spearheads into its jaws. It may be possible to tie the rawhide cord to a tree to keep the crocodile from heading back into the water. Then we'll be able to see if our spears can penetrate the hard protective plates."

The hunters were watching with great interest. Sim continued, "I also have made four extra-heavy flint axes with the heads about twice the size of the usual ones. They are chipped so that the blade resembles a

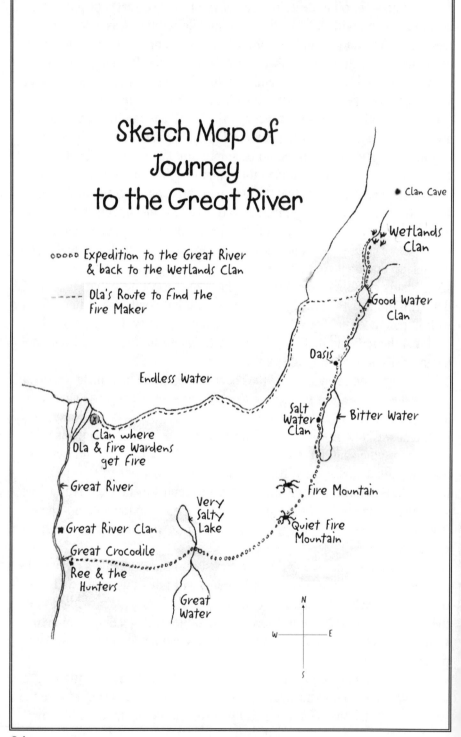

Sketch Map of Journey to the Great River

Clan Cave

Wetlands Clan

ooooo Expedition to the Great River & back to the Wetlands Clan

----- Ola's Route to Find the Fire Maker

Good Water Clan

Oasis

Endless Water

Salt Water Clan

Bitter Water

Clan where Ola & Fire Wardens get Fire

Fire Mountain

Great River

Very Salty Lake

Quiet Fire Mountain

Great River Clan

Great Crocodile

Ree & the Hunters

Great Water

N

W — E

S

spearhead more than an axe head. These should, if anything can, penetrate the heavy hide. But they are heavy. I felt that only Ab and Dedu could use them. At that time I did not know how strong Grew and Sill were."

"If the group decides to go, I wouldn't miss it for anything," said Sill.

"Nor I," said Grew. "The thought makes one feel young again. And I would like to say that I know a shorter route to your people, Ola, than the one you took to get here. Well, do we go? After all the work Sim did for this expedition, it would be a shame to miss it." Grew looked around. Everyone looked eager and nodded "yes." "Then we go," he said.

"Now we have to decide when to go. Food and water will have to be prepared," said Dedu.

"All that's done. We have dried smoked horse meat and enough water bags for each person to have one," said Eevo.

"Then let's start tomorrow," said Sill emphatically. "By the way, who's going?"

"From what I gather, all of you but me," said Seer. "If I were a little younger, you would have trouble keeping me back. Sim claims that he has no trouble with his foot. Besides, he must see if his weapon design is good."

"We are going! Just like that?" exclaimed Ola.

"Just like that," repeated Shim.

Despite Eevo's claim that all was in readiness, there were some last-minute tasks that needed doing. It was mid-morning before the group left for the Great River country. Their first stop would be the Good Water Clan, where Sill told them his people lived on the shore of a fresh-water sea. The sea provided his people with many fish, and the land about the sea was very much like the land of the Wetlands Clan.

"And," he said, looking at the height of the sun in the sky, "we can be there before nightfall."

"Three or four days after we leave Sill's clan, we will be at my home," said Grew. "It's completely different. No trees to be seen. It's also on the shore of a sea, but one that has no life in it. The water is extremely salty, actually bitter. No fish or even insects are found in it. No grasses or reeds grow at its edge. There are only rocks and high cliffs reaching far above. But where we live, great springs of good fresh water pour out of the ground and fall over the cliffside like a veil of water. This water creates an island of green with lots of animal life. The people of the Salt Water Clan have a steady supply of food.

"It will be wonderful to see such things," said Ree. "None of us from our clan have ever been anywhere else, except for Dedu, Eevo and

Sim."

"After that it will be very dry land with very few places that have water, Grew continued. "It was always a dangerous area, not because of predators, but because of the scarcity of water. The water bags that I'm told you and others of your clan made will make travel through those lands much safer. Sim told me how all of you worked, using the stomachs and bladders from the large deer. Eevo now tells me that the sections of the special gut that horses have has made even better ones. We'll see how they work."

Nineteen

A Journey of Surprises

They set off downstream, keeping the river on their right. Sill, being the one who knew the first part of the journey best, led the way along with his two cubs. Some hundreds of paces behind came Grew with his young wolves, Neeth keeping a watchful eye.

Next were Ab, Ree and Og, with their two wolves, one male and one female, from different litters. The river on their right limited the cubs wanderings. Then came Shim and Dedu and two cubs, with Grosh close by. Bringing up the rear were Eevo, Ola and Sim with the remaining two cubs and both Grosh's and Neeth's mates. As Sim and Eevo were the most experienced in communicating with wolves, they held the most vulnerable position. Each group was positioned more than five hundred paces from any other group so that the cubs would get their instructions from only the people they would live with as adults. Evening stops were also to be separate, but close enough so that all the groups could quickly come to the assistance of one another if necessary.

Early in the afternoon they reached the point where the river opened into a very large body of water. They followed the shore of the lake. It was so wide that it was difficult to see the opposite shore. Soon they came to a small river flowing into the lake. They crossed the river and continued to follow the shoreline.

Just before sunset, a call from Sill let the rest know that he was at his clan's home. The groups made camp wherever they were, spread out over a large territory. The cubs stayed with their people, sleeping beside them, but the adult wolves, as always, went out to hunt as a pack of four. Eevo had stayed the night with Sill's cubs. The next morning she found that Sill's mate, a capable-looking woman, had decided that she would accompany Sill. He was worried that the others might not like this, but the three other women welcomed her. She was called Loo. Dedu asked Grew if he too would like to have his mate come along with the group. He, however, told them that his mate had died a few years ago and that he lived alone. The only reason they would have to stop at his clan would be to fill the water bags. This would be the last place they were sure of good water for the next two hands of days, or slightly more.

Leaving Sill's clan caves, the group continued in the direction of the noon sun, always following the coastline. Before noon they came to another river, flowing out of the lake. Grew, who had now become the guide, had stopped and was waiting for the group to join him. He told them that their course was to follow the river toward the very bitter salt lake where his clan lived. The river must be crossed here because his clan lived on the right side of that lake. They ate and continued downstream, this time along the right bank.

The next three days were very much the same, a rushing river and steeply sloping land. The terrain forced the groups closer together. For the time being, they had to abandon the distance between them that they had thought of as ideal. It was while travelling almost in single file that they came to an oasis, a lush area with trees and bushes and plants of all kinds, just a short distance from the river that was hurrying through a desert-like landscape. There were animal tracks to be seen, especially around the many springs that formed little rivulets flowing through the vegetation. But there were no people.

"This would be a wonderful place for a clan site!" Ree exclaimed. "It is far better than anything we have seen. Ab and Og, do you suppose that we could move our clan to this place?"

"There do not seem to be any caves," said Og.

Ab said nothing, but looked about and sampled some berries.

"It is a pleasant place," he said. "Let's make camp here as one group for the rest of the day and night. There are small animals and the cubs could try for a rabbit or so."

Grew agreed. "You won't find anything as pleasant until we get to my clan in three or four days."

Ola, who had overheard Og, said, "There are no caves along the

Great River where I live, yet our clan is at least as big as that of the Wetlands. When we get there, I'll show you how we make our homes. They'd suit a place like this."

By late morning the next day, they came to the end of the river where it emptied into a large lake. The water in the lake did not have the usual wind ripples that they had seen on the lake at Sill's home. The surface looked thick and had little movement. As Grew had said, nothing grew along the shoreline. One of the cubs raced into the water and splashed some over its face. It yelped and tried running out but lost its footing. The cub floated on his side and back, high in the water. Grew waded in slowly to rescue him. He then washed its face and eyes with water from a water bag to remove the stinging salt. That cub, one of the more boisterous, was very subdued that day and kept far away from the lake.

"This is very bad water," Grew said, "but there are places where hot water, with a strong smell, bubbles out of the ground. Some of our people like to soak in those springs. I am one."

They continued following the coastline on their left for the rest of the day and the next one. Nothing was growing. There were large high cliffs on the right-hand side and, across the lake, what appeared to be high mountains. Towards evening of the second day, with all of them hot and uncomfortable, Sim was heard muttering something about why, with so much good land about, anyone would choose to live in so unpleasant a place. Just then they came to the home of the Salt Water Clan and suddenly the air was pleasant.

There was the smell of fresh water and the sound of water falling from high rocks above. Before them was a pool of water, with a group of children standing under a waterfall, the water splashing over them. The sudden intrusion of strangers and wolves startled the young ones. When they saw Grew, the cries stopped, only to be replaced by happy greetings. Grew, it was soon obvious, was to his clan what Seer was to the Wetlands Clan. This was a happy clan, and a safe one. There were almost no predators except for a species of large cat. And these generally hunted prey smaller than people.

In many ways, this was as pleasant a place as the one that had been their resting place three days ago. Everyone, even Dedu, bathed under the waterfall. Grew even convinced Dedu to try the hot springs. He was almost sorry as Dedu did not want to leave. "At last, water that is warm enough for to enjoy," he said, as he finally came out, almost limp from all the hot soaking.

They feasted on berries and other fruits. The water bags were emptied, rinsed and refilled, full this time. They might not have another chance for quite a while. After a reluctant farewell, the group departed. Another two days of travelling alongside the bitter lake brought them to its end. Steadily they had been heading toward the position of the sun at noon. Now they shifted direction, heading towards the point on the horizon where the sun sets in the middle of the cold season, when the daylight is shortest.

As they moved away from the lake, the land began to rise slightly. They travelled through shallow valleys between moderate hills. The land was mostly a chalk base with vast amounts of flint imbedded in it. Sim had never imagined that so much flint existed. He wanted to collect some but there was no way to carry any, not unless he wanted to get rid of the water bag he was carrying. But that would have been foolish, which Sim most certainly was not. So he marked the area in his mind — perhaps on the way back.

One night, three days later, Eevo, Shim and Loo were looking at the lights in the sky when Eevo spotted a glow in the distance, right on the horizon line. It lay along the route they were taking. It was similar to the glimmer of light that she and Sim had seen from the cliff top over their cave which had led them to their parents. The glow was red to yellow in colour while the sky lights were white.

"I wonder whose fire that can be," she said as they all looked in the direction of the light.

"You're looking at the fire mountain," said Grew, who had come up behind them. "I once had to climb it to get fire, about one hand of years ago. That was when all of us had lost all our fires — my clan, the Wetlands and the Good Water clans. It was a horrifying experience. I had two companions, one of whom was my young brother. He lived with the Wetlands Clan and was Kno's mate. Mee looks and acts so much like him, when he was a young boy. They both died on the mountainside when some of the smoke from the mountain passed over them. I was off to one side and escaped. Each of us had managed to light a branch from the hot rock that had poured out of the mountain and were just on our way down. One moment we were all excited that we had a new fire, the next moment they were dead. There were no wounds, but they were dead." He smiled sadly at Eevo. "Now, thanks to you, all that is in the past."

Eevo was shocked. "They were just borrowing some fire and died for it!" she exclaimed. "This fire mountain killed them? Why? What is a fire mountain, anyway?"

"It is a mountain. This one is not a very large one. Sometimes, it makes very loud rumbling noises. Sometimes it even shakes the earth.

100

Whenever this happens, it is very scary. Sometimes there are clouds of smoke coming from the top. Sometimes large red hot rocks are thrown in the air and then they roll down from the top. Sometimes thick rivers of something very hot flow down its sides and become very hot rocks. It was from one of those rivers that we lit our branches."

"So that is what Mee told us. She said that her mother had no mate because a mountain had killed him. She couldn't understand how," remembered Sim.

Grew took charge, "The fire mountain is in an angry mood. It is best that I lead us around it, staying far away. Some three days further there is another fire mountain, but I have never seen it awake. If it is still quiet we may be able to look at it more closely."

The following morning the group found everything, including themselves covered in grey ash. The sky was a dull grey. The sun did not shine through the airborne ash. They left as quickly as possible and changed their course to take them away from the mountain. Occasionally, there were sounds like distant thunder and twice the ground underfoot trembled. For the first time in Eevo or Sim's experience, the wolves were frightened and unsure of themselves. As the day wore on and as the distance between them and the mountain increased, everyone began to feel better. Conditions returned to normal. That evening as the sky darkened, the normal lights seen in the sky appeared ahead of them, but the sky behind was dark with an occasional flare of reddish light.

The next two days were uneventful but travelling continued through a landscape that was still unpleasant. There was always the danger of getting lost. The ravines between the rugged cliffs sometime ended suddenly, so that more than once they had to go back to take a different route. Then the land began to climb. Grew said that they were on the slope of the quiet fire mountain.

Sim had been walking rather slowly as his left ankle was not suited for climbing that steep a slope. He was watching the ground ahead carefully. Suddenly, he ran ahead, stopped, then stooped down. He began to dig into a heap of rubble. Eevo and Ola turned and ran toward him, not knowing what had happened. They found an excited Sim busily excavating a quantity of black stone.

"This is the hard black rock that splits into the sharpest blades. I never have seen so much of it. And such good rock. There's enough here to make the finest knives and spearheads for the entire clan. I must take it with me!" exclaimed Sim.

"How will you carry it?" asked Ola. "We're already carrying as much equipment as we can. Let's remember this spot. On our way back, when we're not so loaded, we can pick it up and take it back. Seer will be happy."

"Yes," said Eevo, "and look, there's some more. The whole hill is covered with them."

"All right," said Sim, "but I will take enough for a few tools. On the way back I'll get all of you to carry as much as you can." He picked up four smaller flawless pieces of the black obsidian and put them into his neck pouch.

The three returned to following Grew, quickly closing the gap between them. This fire mountain was not high. Upon reaching the top, they looked down into the hole of the old crater. Grew did not want any of them to enter and none of the rest particularly wanted to explore it. The wolves did run down the crater slopes, but as there was nothing there to interest them, they came back quickly when called.

Two days after leaving the quiet fire mountain, the land was once again suitable for each group to be separated from the others. As Dedu and Shim, with their cubs and with Grosh's mate as lead wolf, entered a ravine, the wolf suddenly stopped. He crouched down, hackles up, and began to back away, then turned and ran to Dedu. Dedu had hunted with this wolf and understood his signals. He moved up to where the wolf waited. Then, followed closely by Dedu, the wolf climbed a small hill. The wind blowing toward him brought a smell neither liked, the rank smell of a big predator. As they cleared the rise Dedu could see what had turned the wolf back. There, overlooking the game trail that Dedu's group had been following, was a pride of lions, one male and three females and three young cubs. They were waiting to attack whatever was using the trail. The lions knew that prey was coming, but were not aware that they had been seen.

As Dedu and the wolf came down off the small slope, he signalled the other groups. Already they had started to move together. The hunters talked.

"We can avoid those lions," said Sill.

"Yes," said Dedu. "But by now they probably know that we are here. They can follow us. We're probably not in any danger, but the cubs most certainly are. We must get rid of them. But there's great danger in any meeting with animals as powerful as four adult lions. How can we do it without actually fighting them? Ab, Sim, Eevo — you have had experience in these things. How can we do this?"

"Ask Sim or Eevo," replied Ab. "They are likely to have an idea." Eevo turned the question to Sim. He rose to the challenge and began. "Well, Seer said that the crocodile never being hunted had no good defenses. A pride of four lions probably has never been hunted either. Let's try to confuse them. But let's not be really skillful hunters. If we begin an obvious stalk of them, and from a number of different directions, they'll soon realize that they are the prey. Once that happens, if we are lucky, they will try to escape. But we must be ready to fight if they don't. We must have some burning torches as fire is our best weapon. Dedu, you are the clan hunt master, plan the hunt. Think of them not as lions but as horses. Better yet as elk. Elk can be dangerous animals and can attack."

"Good," agreed Dedu. "They're elk. We must let them know that we are trying to drive them. Eevo, you and Sim and Ola light a fire and make up torches. When we have them, Sill, Sim and I, with Grosh's mate and four cubs, will advance along the game trail. As soon as we see them, we will move towards them. Shim, Loo and Ab, you come from over that small rise. Take Grosh and two cubs. Make sure that your torches are very evident and, if you can, smoky."

The others were to go behind the lions and come at them from different directions. Torches were prepared and, at Dedu's signal, they moved out.

Once the lions saw the group they were waiting for, they began their stalk. Knowing that the wolf/people group had seen them, the lions were waiting for their prey to panic and run. When that happened, they could pick off whichever was the easier catch. But it did not. Instead the intended prey swung toward the lions and continued to advance. Suddenly, a similar group topped the little slope on the lions' right. It too was advancing on the pride. The lions were confused. Their hunt was not going well. The lions broke off their stalk and moved to their left, but another force of wolf and people was coming from that direction. There was the smell of smoke. The lions began to retreat and tried to leave as a pride by moving further to the left. But then the fourth group of people carrying fire was moving in from that direction. The male was the first to break. He ran off in a panic, followed by the three females and trailed by the yearling cubs. Reaching open country, they made good their escape.

As their group came back together, Dedu spoke: "I don't think that pride will follow us hoping to pick up stragglers."

Ahead lay open sandy country. Shim, in the lead, pointed to the sky ahead. "Look! Birds!" she said. "I haven't seen any since we left Grew's clan." Just over the hill, a lake shimmered in the sunlight.

Twenty

Crocodile: The Great One

"I know where we are!" exclaimed Ola. "That's the salt lake. We can cross between that lake and a huge salt sea that lies about a day's trip toward the noon sun. My people are about three days straight ahead, on the bank of the Great River."

Dedu had a request. "Before meeting your people, I would like to go to the Great River, somewhere without people. I want time to see what I can of crocodiles."

"Then we should go a little up river," said Ola. "Up river there are many places with crocodiles, water mammoths and other animals. As a rule, people stay away from these beasts. Sometimes hunters come for water birds and small deer, but we'll have plenty of warning of danger. The wolves will give us that. But we have to do something about the cubs. They're still cubs. They'll want to play in the river. Crocodiles could take them easily."

"You're right. But how can we keep them away from the water?" asked Dedu.

Ree spoke up. "As we've travelled, I've come to know them, and I'm not the hunter the rest of you are. I get along best with Neeth. Perhaps she and I could take the cubs away from the group. We'd need a suitable place before we get too close to the river. I think that Neeth and I could keep them out of harm's way for a few days."

Ree's suggestion was a good one. They would try it. After they head from Ola's home, Ree, Neeth and all the cubs separated from the rest. One of the small wooded areas a short distance from the river looked like a safe place for the cubs, far away from crocodiles. The others continued to the river.

Neeth's mate was uncertain as to where he wanted to go. Sim gave him the signal to go with Neeth. Ree and Neeth would have eight five-moon-old cubs to keep in check. Another adult wolf might prove useful. Besides, Sim could not see how an additional wolf would be of help in the hunt for a huge and mostly aquatic predator like the crocodile.

By noon they were in sight of the Great River. Ola had not exaggerated. It was enormous. The river looked quite peaceful, but they approached with great caution. This was unknown territory, with an unknown opponent.

At the riverbank, they glanced up and down, looking for anything unusual. Quite a few wading birds were in the shallows, and further upriver a number of deer-like animals called impala were drinking. Grosh's mate took a wide swing around and behind the unsuspecting animals. Suddenly, aware of the wolf, the impala panicked and scattered. One entered the water. There was a sudden explosion as a large body surfaced and massive toothed jaws grabbed the fleeing animal. Despite the struggles of the impala, it was dragged below the surface, leaving only an ripple in the water that soon subsided. The wolf, Grosh's mate, backed off and rejoined the party. All were a little subdued, and much impressed by the swift, unanticipated attack.

"I have always known that people were not meant to go into water," said Dedu grimly. "Now I know why. It's just as well that none of the cubs are here. We know there's at least one crocodile here in the water!"

Carefully, they all examined the surface of the water near them. Then Ab said excitedly, "I can see one, no, two, no, a number of them! Look for two little spots floating on the water close together and two other spots about a forearm's length away, a little farther apart. I am going to try to hit one with a stone." His aim was good. They were rewarded by a flurry in the water. When a huge head came to the surface, they speedily backed away from the edge of the water. The large head sank again. Soon all to be seen were the four little bumps on the surface, the two nostrils and two eyes. Altogether, they could identify at least four, maybe six crocodiles.

"If these are the smaller ones that congregate together, how big are

106

the solitary ones?" wondered Sill. "Will the spears be strong enough?"

Sim took a number of pieces of smoked meat and tied them together in a small bundle. He threw it into the water and waited. For a moment nothing happened, then two of the crocodiles swam for it. There was a short struggle and one snatched the meat. He repeated his experiment, but this time tied the meat to a long piece of thin rawhide that he had brought from Shim's supply at home. This time, once the meat hit the water, he pulled it ashore. A crocodile about as long as two men charged out of the water, grabbed the meat and pulled it back into the river.

"Good! That's what I needed to know," said Sim. "Let's try to find a large one. I have a plan."

The entire group worked their way upstream, carefully searching the water for any evidence of a solitary crocodile. A fair amount of time passed with no results. Finally, a little ahead of them, they heard the sound of a large body entering the water. Wavelets washed up on the shore. Whatever it was, it was big! Ab remarked that it had probably heard them coming. Likely it had entered the water with the intent of awaiting them and, if possible, taking one of them as prey.

"We will not co-operate, if that is its intention," exclaimed Grew. "Let's move back and watch." After much looking, Ab again spotted the telltale nostrils and eyes. They were much farther apart than those in the other stretch of water. The hunters and the crocodile spent some time watching each other, neither making any move. Finally, for some reason, the crocodile approached the shore, climbed out of the water and lay down at the water's edge. Before long it was difficult not to see it as a large tree trunk that had been carried down by the river's current and beached on shore.

Shim broke the silence. "It's almost sunset. We now know where it lives. No other animal is likely to scare that giant from its home. Let's eat and make plans for tomorrow."

Og and the wolves went hunting and brought back a young impala, which would provide the wolves, the hunters, and, tomorrow if all went well, the crocodile, with a meal. The crocodile's meal, they hoped, would not be easy to digest. After sunset they ate and went to sleep beside their fire, far away from the water. No one knew how far the crocodile could travel.

In the morning, picking up all the equipment they would need, the group returned to the place the crocodile had been the previous day. The rawhide attached to the double-headed spear was laid out so that it would feed out freely. Next the remains of the impala were fastened on the two

107

spearheads. The long pole handle that grasped the shaft of the baited two-headed spear was attached and checked to make sure it would release when required. All was in readiness. Now where was that crocodile?

There were no telltale bumps floating on the surface of the river. They looked up and down river, examining the banks carefully. No crocodile to be found. Then Ola pointed to a section of tree trunk far up the bank, more than half buried in the mud.

"Was that here yesterday?" he asked.

"It's almost buried," said Sim. "It can't be the crocodile. It most certainly is an old log."

Just then Grosh's mate came running along the bank, spraying mud and water. A frustrated Sim mumbled, "We should have sent all the wolves away with Ree. This is one hunt where they're not helpful. They're actually in the way. Hunting an animal like this crocodile is a purely human thing."

Grosh's mate continued running back and forth along the bank. He would come closer to the buried log then race back a bit. Then Grosh joined in the fun, doing much the same.

"I hope they don't get too close to the water. That crocodile may be hiding anywhere. I wish those wolves weren't here!" exclaimed Sim.

Now the two wolves charged the log. This time they did not stop. The log exploded, hurling mud everywhere as huge jaws snapped for Grosh. But Grosh was not there. She had changed her run and leaped over the crocodile. Then her mate did the same. The crocodile whirled around faster than the hunters thought possible for such a large and sluggish-looking an animal. As fast as it was, it might as well have been moving at a walk as far as the two wolves were concerned. Their muscles and reflexes were far better. Besides, they could keep this up for a half day or more. Before long, the crocodile was beginning to tire. It was frustrated and very angry. Time after time, it bellowed and charged, but caught only air. But with every charge, it moved further away from the river.

"Look!" cried Eevo, "they are herding it, keeping it away from the water. It's time we joined in."

Grabbing her favourite slender spear with its sharp obsidian point, she ran toward the crocodile. Dropping the point of her spear so that the point was over the animal's upper chest wall, she used her spear as in the game of spear jumping and drove the spear point almost through the animal's chest as she cleared the crocodile's body. Eevo landed on its far side and rolled out of range of the massive tail. Up to now, the crocodile had only been angered by the wolves, but now it was hurt and desperate to get back to the river.

Ab had been watching, dumbfounded, as Eevo attacked. He too knew the game. It had been started by the young people of his clan. Now it was his turn as the crocodile tried to turn. Ab's spear was one of the special ones that Sim had made for the crocodile hunt. It was made to cut as many blood vessels as possible, and Ab's weight was at least twice Eevo's. That spear penetrated deeply.

Now the crocodile wanted only to escape. Having turned toward the river, it was dragging itself along when Dedu ran alongside. He swung his heavy axe with its pick-like point and struck at the spot where the spinal cord leaves the brain. Despite the heavy protective plates, the sharp point crushed the massive backbone and severed the crocodile's spinal cord. Its tail twitched once. Then the animal went limp. The monster that could not be killed was dead.

As they stood in amazement at what they had done, and so easily, they became aware of Neeth and her mate. Looking up, they saw Ree, the wolf cubs and three strange men watching them.

Twenty-One

Strange Men

Ree, Neeth and the cubs started toward the forested area to their left. Neeth kept looking back and sometimes stopped and waited. At first Ree did not understand why, but then she saw Neeth's mate coming at a quick lope. At first she thought that this would complicate things. Then, realizing how difficult it could get if the cubs were suddenly to scatter, she felt that another fast-moving, responsible adult wolf would be very welcome.

She intended to make this side trip a rest period. There would be some hunting and training, but they would stay there until the others came back to get them. Perhaps this rest would also give her a chance to think about what would be needed if the clan could be persuaded to move to that wonderful oasis they had found. In her mind she could see the far easier life that would await them there.

They entered the cool shade of the tree canopy while Neeth and her mate explored the area. As they seemed to like it, she had no qualms about giving the cubs free rein. She looked to see if there were any caves, but in this sandy soil there were none. Using her knife, she trimmed some tree boughs and made a small shelter near a stream that flowed from some place a little higher. The cubs hunted for rodents while Neeth and her mate kept a watchful eye. "Neeth's mate should have a name," she thought to herself. "Dog, I'll call him Dog."

After the many days of travel in dry country with almost no greenery, it was pleasant to be here. She hoped the others were safe and able to find the crocodile. Getting out her fire-making tools, she soon had a good small fire going. It was not necessary to hunt as she had plenty of food, and the nearby stream would provide plenty of good water.

So Ree sat and ate, slept a little and was completely relaxed. The sun set and she thought, "Here I am alone in the woods at night. Twelve moons ago I would have been so frightened. Somewhere close at hand are two large wolves and nine five-moon-old cubs. They are my friends and they will protect me, just as I will them. I am not the frightened girl I was a year ago. I carry a sharp knife and two hunting spears. And I know how to use them. I have a mate, a pleasant man and just about the best hunter in our, or any, clan. I have friends who are capable of anything and I am a Keeper of the Fire. How I have changed! I like this me far better." Soon she fell asleep.

The next morning Ree woke and ate, then went looking for berries. This was the right time of year for them. As the sun got higher she began to wonder about the others. How were things going?

Unexpectedly, her attention was brought back to her surroundings. Neeth was at her side, touching her hand. Ree allowed herself to be led toward the edge of the wood. In the distance she saw three men approaching. They looked like hunters. The men carried spears that had very white tips, not grey or black like those made by Sim and Seer. Neeth was not sure how to treat these strangers. Ree, too, was unsure. She knew that they were in other people's territory. This could well be the hunting ground of these people. If so, then she was the stranger. Her many moons as Keeper of the Fire had taught her to trust in her own judgement. And so she decided that there was nothing to be lost in being friendly. There was no need to let the others know what her strengths and her weakness were either.

Ree signalled the wolves to stay hidden, a signal well understood by the cubs. By now, although still young, they were a respectable size, about one-third to one-half the weight of a full-grown wolf or a large man. The wolves disappeared as if they had melted into the bushes. She went back to her fire and waited.

Ree was right. Although she did not know it, they were hunters from Ola's home. They were looking for some of the impala that lived along the river and often found in these small sheltered areas along the river valley. So far they had not been successful. As they approached, they could smell smoke. This surprised them. How could there be fire? This was an unpopulated area. Fire was found only in the sites where there were Fire Wardens. No one else was allowed to touch or look after fire. Perhaps this was one of those special sites where fire from the sky had landed. They were puzzled. Just where was that smoke coming from? What would they find? Just as they were getting close, they heard what sounded like a human voice, but one speaking in a language they did not understand. The voice sounded as if from a woman! Pushing though the shrubbery, they found a young woman sitting in front of a neatly-made fire. She reached into the fire and carefully took out a burning branch which she held out to them.

"Welcome. Please come and share my fire," invited Ree.

She knew they did not understand her language but they should, she felt, have understood her tone and gesture. Instead they staggered back in horror. A woman touching fire! It was one of the greatest crimes in their society. The Chief Fire Warden must be informed. The woman must be taken before the Council of Wardens for punishment. All three began to shout, "Why did you do it? Who's with you? How did you get the fire?"

While Ree did not understand the words, the tone of voice and the gestures were unmistakable. She stood up and picked up her spear. This brought laughter from the men.

"She is making matters worse," said one "A woman with a weapon. Why, it's so thin as to be useless. Come, we'll teach her a lesson, then take her to the Chief Fire Warden."

Their threatening way of speaking was familiar to Ree. The same unpleasant tone of voice had been used by some of the nastier older boys and men before she became a Keeper of the Fire whenever she had done something to displease them. Sometimes they just wanted to hit her. They did it because they were stronger and there were more of them. That was many yesterdays ago. This was now. This Ree was not going to allow such behaviour.

Ree raised her spear so that the sharp flint rested in the little notch where a person's neck rises from the chest. The sharp tip drew a drop of blood which trickled down the chest of the man who was in the central position. He gasped and stepped back. The other two also stepped back and tried to raise their spears, but were unsuccessful. At a motion of Ree's hand, Neeth and Dog each leaped at one of the men, knocking them down. The standing man found himself facing a very sharp spear. The weapon he had called a toy just moments ago had changed in his mind to what it was - a very deadly spear held by someone who knew how to use it. The two on the ground found themselves with the fangs of a wolf just a thumb's width from each of their throats. The laughter and bravado displayed just a moment ago were gone, replaced by frightened moans. With good reason

113

they were too terrified to move.

Ree knelt down and picked up their three spears. She checked, but they had no knives. Stepping back, she told the wolves to let them up. Now, what was she to do with these men? It might be dangerous for the cubs, but Ree felt that she had to re-establish communication with the rest of her group. She instructed the wolves to herd the three men and to follow her.

All headed towards the river, led by a confident Ree. The three captives began to consider Ree as not human. After a long period of travel, they began to talk. The woman did not seem to mind, so they continued.

"She talks to wolves and they understand her," said one. "The way she had that spear at my neck shows that she has done it before," said the one who had found out how sharp it was.

"I don't think the Fire Warden would be happy to meet that one," said the third. "I wonder where she is taking us?"

"We appear to be going toward the river," noted the leader of the three. "She seems quite pleasant now, not at all angry. Come to think of it, she never got angry. She seems to be completely confident." The three were truly dumbfounded by this behaviour from a woman.

The leader found his bearings. "We're getting close to the river, near at the pool of the Great One. Look! Something's going on down there. There are more people and more wolves. The Great One is out of the water . He seems angry. He'll eat the wolves. Probably some of those people too. But they don't act afraid! They must not know how terrible the Great One is. If they were not strangers and connected to this woman, I would feel sorry for them."

Ree and the three men stopped, as did the cubs at Ree's command. The two large wolves, however, raced toward the river to join the others there. Nine smaller wolves made sure that the three men were not about to do anything. The young woman stood and watched. She did not seem concerned about the fate that was to overtake those on the riverbank. Perhaps she did not know them. The Great One would soon have a large store of food in his pool.

But amazingly the wolves below were not running from the Great One . They seemed to be teasing him. "They're fast!" exclaimed one hunter. "He can't seem to catch them."

To their amazement, a young woman, a rather tall one, ran forward carrying a spear, also a light one. Were these women not afraid of anything? Surely they can't be people. What are they? She ran toward the Great One and thrust her spear toward him. His plates will stop that feeble spear, they were certain. But wait, she has launched herself through the air, holding her spear against the monster hide. She rolled free, missed completely by the tail. But the spear was not deflected. It remained deep in the Great One's back.

Once again, right before their eyes, a large Man did the same leaping, but this time with a heavy spear. He went over and rolled back onto his feet. Now there were two spears in that great back. The hunters could scarcely believe their eyes. The young woman who had captured them seemed very pleased. Now a third, even larger man, ran forward carrying a club. A club against that killer of many men, ridiculous! He swung his club and brought it down on that impenetrable hide. The Great One twitched and stopped There were cheers below. The Great One no longer moved. Could it be that it is dead? That men killed him? No, that can't be! These can't be human people. They must be something else that only looks human. They are looking up here! What will they do with us?

Ree moved the group down towards the river.

Twenty-Two

Dealing With Difference

Dedu was fairly bursting with pride. "Did you see that spear vault of Eevo's and then Ab's? I don't know if I would trust a spear shaft to carry my weight like that. To think that Eevo would start something like that!"

Ree and the others had never heard Dedu talk so much. They knew that he must be very excited. Sim brought their attention back to Ree's arrival, "Who are those men with you?"

"I don't know. But they are the reason we're here," she replied. "Neeth told me that they were coming. I tried to welcome them and offered them a part of my fire. For some reason, at that point, they threatened me. I had to disarm them with the help of Neeth and Dog." She hastened to explain, "I named him Dog as I felt he should have a name. But I'm afraid that I had to nick the throat of their leader with my spear."

Ola started to laugh, "Eevo told me that you were always extremely kind and considerate. Now you show yourself to be so aggressive. Excuse my laughing, but now that it is over, with no one hurt, your adventure is very funny. Let me explain."

Ola knew these hunters were men from his clan. Immediately, he knew how the misunderstanding arose between them and Ree. The hunters, following what they had been taught, believed that what they were doing was right. Ola continued his explanation to Ree. "You offered them fire. In our society it is considered a crime, an insult for a woman to be near a fire with no Fire Warden present. A woman must never touch fire, or any tools used in the care of fire. The second thing that a woman must never do is handle weapons. You not only had a spear, but you slightly wounded one of them. So you see, to them you were a very wicked woman. In their minds it was their duty to capture you and take you to the Fire Warden's council for punishment."

Ola faced the men and told them how fortunate they were that Ree had taken charge. If they had touched Ree, the wolves would have killed them. The group saw the men's faces pale as they realized how close they had come to losing their lives. Ola then went on to tell these hunters why the group was there. He talked about Sim and his development of new hunting weapons for his clans, the Wetlands, the Good Water, the Salt Water and the old Cave clans — all of them. Ola knew that all this news would get back in some form to the Chief Fire Warden. He went on to explain that Sim needed a very formidable opponent to test the weapons on. That opponent was the crocodile.

Much to the men's surprise, Sim addressed them in their language. He told them that his weapons had proved to be so effective that he had not been able to test all of them. Did they know where another large crocodile could be found? They were not sure. The Great One had kept its large area free of any rivals.

Then Eevo, the first attacker of the Great One, spoke to them. She told them that she was the woman the Sun itself had chosen and taught how to make new fires whenever they were needed. She said she had promised the Sun that she would teach anyone who wanted to learn. The Sun wanted its gift spread and did not want any one group controlling this wonderful tool.

Sim continued, saying that he would be happy to give their stronger hunters some of his spears. The defeat of the crocodile had proven that these weapons had no trouble getting through the tough crocodile plates and hide.

The three hunters stood silently, waiting for what they had heard to make sense to them. These new human beings, so strong that they used monsters like the Great One as playthings to test their weapons, were offering them these same weapons. And also the unheard-of gift, control of fire, so that they could have fire on their hunts for warmth and protection. All they had to do was to continue teaching others the skills required. This would mean freedom from the control of the council of Fire Wardens.

From being prisoners just minutes ago, they now had the offer of

118

gifts that they could not even have imagined before. They turned to Ola, whom they now recognized as one of the more helpful and pleasant Fire Wardens from their clan. They asked him to seek forgiveness from Ree for their actions. They wanted him to tell her that they had acted according to the rules of their society. But that was still not an excuse for the way they had threatened her, laughed at her and shouted.

In response, Ree turned to them, smiled and nodded. The men realized that they really were free. Immediately, the three went to see the remains of the huge crocodile. It was immense. They looked and felt the two spears firmly imbedded in that great back. They looked at the smashed back plates and fragments of bone where Dedu's axe had struck. Somehow, no matter what these people said, it didn't seem that they could be human. But they were friendly. And they had offered wonderful gifts.

The entire group then tried to turn the crocodile over, after the spears had been removed. But they found that, as soon as they got one part turned and moved to another part, the first would slip back. Finally, using spear shafts as levers and their rope to hold the part they had moved, they were successful. The head of the Great One was removed. It was to be taken to the clan living area to convince any doubters and, of course, the Chief Fire Warden, that this was a strong group whose requests it might be wise to allow.

It took four people to carry the huge head. Two of the heavy spears were pushed through the mouth and out at the cut-off neck, giving them handles for carrying purposes. They had all the other equipment to carry too, so having three extra people was helpful. By evening they reached the area of the Great River Clan and made camp just outside the settled area. The three hunters watched this experienced group quickly settle, then watched in fascination as Eevo started a fire. This they had never seen before. Now they hurried away to report, but went to their fellow hunters rather than to the Wardens as they should have done according to clan rules.

The newcomers explored their new surroundings. They saw no signs of anything like a cave. Instead, there were strange-looking structures within an enclosure made of what looked like bushes. Ola told them that the enclosure was made of thorn bushes. Wherever the openings in this enclosure were, there was a large fire burning with a man standing near. They counted one hand and three fingers of fires. "Those are Fire Wardens watching their fires," said Ola.

It had been a most incredible day. Everyone was suddenly very sleepy. They lay down on their mats, feeling safe as always when the wolves were with them.

Twenty-Three

A Reunion

The story that the three hunters told was passed from mouth to mouth. With each telling, it changed and grew. The story that reached the Council of Wardens was of a large group of very powerful hunters, who had come from far away. This group included women hunters as well as men. All of them could, when they wished to, take on the shape of wolves. The women in the group could make fire, any time they chose. They also carried special spears capable of piercing any substance. The one woman that the three hunters met first, and unwittingly offended, had turned herself into two great wolves and knocked the hunters down. The woman part of her had actually thrust her spear into the throat of the group's leader. She had disarmed them and driven them to the pool of the Great One. There the hunters had seen the Great One being taunted by two hunters in their wolf shape. The young woman who was the one who had talked to the Sun, and who was his messenger and the chief Fire Maker, had floated up into the air and then thrust her spear through the Great One, killing him. They had then cut off the Great One's head and brought it with them. This group were now camped just outside the clan area. They had with them a Fire Warden. This was the Fire Warden who had not returned with the other Fire Wardens when they brought back fire to replace the fire put out by the high waters of the Great River.

"That must be Ola," the Chief Warden said to the Deputy Chief. "That is good news. But he is a headstrong young troublemaker. I was afraid that he had died after deserting his group to go on a useless chase."

He turned to another of the wardens and ordered, "Take a party of hunters and bring him to me. I would like to speak with him, in here, alone."

The deputy went out and called a group of hunters whose job it was to enforce the Chief Warden's orders. But they, by now, knew about the magical powers of the strangers and their weapons. They had also seen the wolves. "No," they answered. "We are not going against that group."

The Chief Warden, when informed, was very angry. But there was nothing he could do at the time. Instead he told his deputy to get all the information that he could about why Ola left his group that spring. Both of them had heard the stories that were being told, especially those mentioning women making fire. But they also knew how much hunters could exaggerate, and did not pay much attention.

"That young man has caused me much concern and trouble," the Chief muttered to himself. "I hope he has learned that there is no such thing as a fire maker. Fire comes only from other fires or from fire mountains, or perhaps sometimes from the flashes of light from the sky during storms with much thunder. He knows that I am angry with what he has done. But he came back. I wonder why?" A little feeling of unease began to enter his thoughts for the first time. Could Ola have been right? Even so, he should not have gone alone.

All the people who had been on the fire-getting trip and the three hunters who had been with this strange group were brought to the Chief Warden. He wanted to know who the strangers were and what they wanted. Why was Ola with them? What was their interest in Ola?

The following morning Sim woke early, as did the others. They were still excited about their easy victory. Sim wanted to find another large, solitary crocodile. Would his double spear work again? But Ola's problem had to be settled first. They had to be sure that Ola would not be harmed, and that he would be allowed to come and go as he pleased. They had to have a talk with the Chief Warden.

As Sim thought this, Ola turned to him and said, "I think that I should go to the Chief Warden's house and speak to him. I'll tell him that I found the Fire Maker and that she has come to teach the making of fire. I'll tell him we'll leave tools for the hunters and that I plan to go back to the Wetlands Clan."

"Yes," Sim replied, "but not alone."

Ola sighed. "I must have been a great disappointment to the Chief Warden." Suddenly he began to laugh, "Here I am defending the Chief Warden when I always complained about his constant demands that we do good work. I must be seeing things from a different point of view. You know, if I were Chief Warden, I probably would be very much like him. I have nothing to fear from him except that he may try to make me stay. But now, with your weapons and with the fear of losing our fires because of flooding removed, he might not object too much."

Sim looked at his friend thoughtfully. "Ola, you may be too trusting. I dealt with people who, when I was a small child, were supposed to protect me. But when my parents were away, they were happy to put me out to be some hyena's meal." Sim stood up. "It's time to visit the Chief Warden. All of us, including all the wolves will go."

While Ola and Sim had been busy talking to each other, they had not paid any attention to what was going on around them. Suddenly, there was a good deal of excitement in the air. The wolves were growling. Sim could hear Shim, Dedu and Eevo talking to them. They went over to where Eevo, with some help from the four adult wolves, was trying to calm the cubs. Looking up, they saw a group of men approaching their camp. A tall, slender, confident-looking older man was in the lead.

On seeing him, Ola ran forward. The man increased his speed of walking, then he ran toward Ola. When they met, he held his arms extended, and Ola put his arms out. The two embraced in friendship.

"Is this the feared Chief Warden Ola had talked about?" thought Sim. This was not as he had pictured him.

Sim could hear the man say, "Ola, I missed you so much. At first I was hurt that you would leave as you did. Then I was angry, extremely angry, that you, whom I considered so bright, would take so dangerous a trip alone. I thought that you had probably died somewhere. Then my anger passed and only worry and loneliness were left. Last night I heard that a group of unbelievable people had arrived. They were people who had killed the Great Crocodile, the one responsible for many deaths of our people. But the stories also talked about women who could fly and who had the ability to turn into wolves. Such wonders as these I did not believe. But there was also mention of a missing Fire Warden. Suddenly I had a great feeling of joy, hope, and also of unbelief. It is true! You really are here!"

Sim, who had stayed back, could see tears running down the Chief Warden's face. Even Ola's eyes were not dry. Eevo and Shim and Dedu were also close enough to hear what was said. Dedu missed the words, as he spoke little of Ola's language, but he could read the gestures. Shim and

Eevo looked surprised. Was this the frightening man Ola had spoken about?

The rest of that day was spent with the travellers getting to know the clan members. There was little chance of getting Ola alone for any explanation, as there was always someone around trying to speak to him. Consequently, Sim decided to try to get to know as many of the clan people as possible, especially the Chief Warden. Finally able to speak to him alone, he found that this man, whom he thought might harm Ola, was very much like Seer. It was then he discovered that Ola was the son of the Chief Warden's sister. Actually, the Chief wanted Ola, in time, to take over as Chief. "Perhaps that is why I was a little hard on him at times, but I wanted him to be the best he possibly could be," explained the Chief Warden. "Now he tells me that he wants to be a member of your clan. That might be good for him, but I will continue to hope that after a time he will return here."

Towards evening, as the fires at the openings in the thorn wall were prepared for the night, Ola asked the Chief Warden, whose name was Lar, if he would like to meet Eevo again. But this time, not as Eevo, but as the Maker of Fire. There really was a Fire Maker, he told them. She had come back with him to teach fire making to the people of the Great River Clan.

Fire making was a subject that had not been mentioned all day. The deputy looked a little uncomfortable, but Lar said that he would be delighted. First, however, he wanted to clear up a few points. Turning to Eevo, he asked her, "Have you actually spoken with the Sun?"

"No," replied Eevo, "but I have spoken to the Sun. I made a promise to the Sun that I would teach fire making to all who wanted to learn."

Lar smiled at that and said, "Has the Sun ever spoken to you?"

Eevo grinned and said, "No." Lar seemed to be happy with that answer, then encouraged Eevo to tell him what had led her to this remarkable ability.

Eevo brought them out her fire-making tools and prepared and lit a fire. After everyone present had examined the fire board and spinning rod, she did it again.

Lar had listened and watched carefully. "All the Wardens, including my deputy and myself, must learn to do this, as well as any of the people who wish to learn. Will you teach us, Eevo?"

"Gladly," was her answer. "We have brought many fire boards and spinning sticks for that. We hoped that was what you would say."

Lar then turned to Ola and said, "Of all the people on your journey

124

you could have met, you met these ones. Surely the Sun has you under its protection too."

Eevo smiled and said, "I have something I wish to ask. Something that troubles me. If women must not touch fire nor tools used for fire maintenance, why is there no objection to me making fire?"

"There is no such law," answered Lar. "But there is custom. And custom is often stronger than any law. But who could object to the only person who has discovered fire making, making fire? The custom probably started with the Chief Fire Wardens in the past, and their way of choosing fire wardens." He went on to explain that the earlier Chiefs had not wanted to have women as fire wardens as women have babies and babies require a great deal of looking after. Looking after the clan fires was a job that required total attention since the fires were the only defense against predators, especially the great cats. A woman with a child could not do both jobs, so they had stated that a woman could not be a fire warden. As time passed, this original reason had been forgotten and altered. In time the very thought of women and fire became contrary to what was considered normal. In the same way, women carrying and using weapons also fell into a similar situation. There was no law, but custom had made one. "Now with what appears to be a direct intervention of the Sun," he said, "I doubt that anyone will object to women making fire in the future."

For the remainder of the time of their stay, they were guests of the Great River Clan. They stayed for three hands of days. Sim, who was instructing the Great River Clan tool makers in flint knapping, told them about a plentiful source of that best-of-all stone for knives and other tools. He described the beautiful black obsidian that was to be found, only about six day's travel in the direction of the mid-afternoon shadows, on the slopes of the quiet fire mountain. Using the pieces he had taken from there, he showed them how to work the stone into the wonderful sharp tools that would help make the clan safer. And so it was that the clan members learned much from their visitors.

As for the members of the group, there were many things that they too learned. Ree was most interested in the making of houses using clay and the reeds that grow in the river. These very same reeds were also to be found beside the Wetlands river and in the oasis that she liked so much. The clay was worked over the loosely woven reeds and made into blocks that were dried in the summer sunlight. Those blocks were then used to make dwellings which, in the winter, were far warmer than caves.

As for the others, Sim learned how to use bone and not only flint for tools. Bone can be carved into many shapes. One of the most important of these bone instruments he learned to make was the bone needle. Shim was shown how the cord she needed for her weaving could be spun much more easily. Sim got to test his two-headed spear and rope on some smaller crocodiles with good results.

During the time that was spent with the people of the Great River Clan, Ree and Ab had developed a close friendship with Ree's three hunters. These men still puzzled over how it was possible for different people to be completely right and yet completely wrong at the same time. Different beliefs can cause big problems. They had thought they were doing the right thing in attacking Ree. But it was wrong. There was much to learn.

However, having a great desire to explore and not being bound by duty in quite the way the Wardens were, they thought that they could get permission to travel, provided that the remaining hunters could get enough food for the clan. Fish was plentiful, but meat was harder to get. The hunters wished to visit the people of the four clans they had met. They even offered to help if the Old Cave Clan decided to move to the oasis. If they could get the Chief to agree, they thought that they would follow in about a hand's worth of moons. Grew promised to mark the route as far as his clan. Dedu would mark it to the Wetlands. The markers were to be a number of flat rocks stacked, three rocks for each mark. Once the markers were in place over the open country, and with specific landmarks in the more rugged parts, travel would be much easier.

Twenty-Four

Heading Home

It was time to leave. Now that Eevo and Sim and the whole group were familiar with the route, and knew where water was to be found, it was considered safe to leave three water bags for others to use. Having accomplished all they had set out to do, the morning for departure came.

The Chief, his deputy and the three hunters, as well as many of the people, including the children who would miss their wolf friends, stood and watched the procession of humans and wolves moving off in the direction of the rising sun. "We will see each other again," each one thought, "maybe next year."

As for the homeward-going group, it had been a great and memorable adventure. Much had been learned and taught. Each member of the party was sorry to be leaving, yet, at the same time, happy to be going home. Ree was, in her mind, planning the move to the wonderful oasis with its good and plentiful water, the fruit and berries in abundance and the edible grass seeds that grew there. No one would have to go hungry in this place and there were no large predators. In her mind she could see her clan changing from a group of suspicious, almost sullen people to one of helpful people like those in the clans she had visited on this trip. Ab too was thinking of the move, if the people could be persuaded. He knew how difficult it was to convince people to change even when the change was so much for the better. He knew that as soon as any difficulty was encountered the people would turn against the move.

Grew was thinking that he was lucky to come from a small but happy clan. The Great River Clan was far larger but he could see that there was not the family feel to it that there was to his small clan. The hunters resented the Fire Wardens' leadership but were not willing to take part in the running of the clan. The Fire Wardens, in their turn, showed that they considered the hunters to be inferior. Well, maybe that would change now. The Good Water Clan was like his, a small but advanced society. It seemed better to keep clans from becoming too large. Only the Wetlands Clan seemed to be able to grow without being spoiled. That, Grew felt, was due to the leadership of Seer and his making sure that everyone in the clan had an important role to play in the running of the clan.

Dedu had reached that conclusion a long time ago. He and the wolves were enjoying the trip. There was no living creature that they needed to fear. What a great change from just a few years back when being a good hunter meant being able to steal some larger animal's kill! Shim, too, was delighted with what she had learned, especially with the making of a needle.

Ola was just happy. He now knew that the Chief Fire Warden was someone who liked him. He had been critical because he wanted Ola to do well. Actually, Ola knew that he had always wanted his chief's approval. Now that he was free to return to the Wetlands Clan, he was also free to go back to his home clan. It was good to belong to more than one group.

Eevo and Sim were gladly going home. In their minds, they were going over how they could use the things they had learned. There were so many things to do. Sim was thinking about Seer's delight with the great amount of obsidian they would bring back. And they had Ola back. Eevo felt a wonderful glow spread through her body at that thought.

Glossary

Aggressive: Very forceful, ready to attack.

Apparition: The appearance of something unlikely or ghostly.

Aquatic: Something that lives in water.

Caecum: A pouch at the beginning of the large bowel or colon. It is very large in horses and in other grasseaters like the zebra. In people it is very small, and is really the appendix.

Canopy: A cover overhead, such as a forest canopy of branches or a canopy of stars in the sky.

Dominance: Power exerted over others. Here it refers to the female wolves establishing their leadership over their mates.

Elk: The largest member of the deer family, called moose in North America.

Entrails: Internal organs of any animal, the guts, plus kidneys and spleen.

Fire boards
and spindles: The best are made from Balsam fir.

Formidable: Difficult to deal with.

Formidable
opponent: A difficult rival; one who is likely to beat you.

Game-trail: A path frequently used by animals for some essential reason.

Grasses: The grasses for spinning to make cords are a variety of flax.

Horses: The horses in this story are quite different from the horses we know today. They were about the size of a small pony, with a short upright mane and rather short and slender legs. There are 174 cave paintings of horses found in the Ariège Valley caves in France, believed to date back to around 28,000 years ago. The breed most closely resembling this prehistoric horse is the Przewalski horse, a subspecies of modern horse, which has disappeared from the wilds of Asia. The very few that are left are found only in captivity.

Hyena:	The striped hyena is found in northeast Africa and Asia Minor extending into the Caucasus mountains. Now an endangered species with only a small number. About the size of a dog, each weighs about 30 kilos. Not to be confused with the large spotted hyena, about 70 kilos in weight, of the South Sahara region.
Knapper:	A Dutch word meaning a stone chipper or flint worker.
Knoll:	A small round hill.
Obsidian:	A jet-black volcanic glass. When broken, it has extremely sharp edges.
Outcrop:	Rock sticking out of the ground.
Pride of lions:	A family or group of lions.
Rise:	A slight elevation of land. A small hill, not rounded like a knoll.
Rodents:	The family of gnawing animals with large upper teeth that continue to grow. Mice, squirrels, rats and beavers are all rodents.
Sacred:	Worthy of worship.
Stalk:	A deliberately slow pursuit of a prey, with the intent to catch and usually kill for food.
Taunt:	Provoke, ridicule or tease in a hurtful way.
Tier:	A series of things in layers, one above another and side by side. The Wetlands caves were set in tiers
Water Mammoth:	A name for the hippopotamus.
Wolf, wolves:	The largest weigh 60 to 80 kilos. They are a member of the dog family, much like the wolves of Russia and Canada. Believed to be the ancestor of our domestic dogs.

About the Author

Henry Shykoff's family came to Canada from Poland when Henry was six years old. He grew up in Toronto and graduated from the University of Toronto medical school in 1949. Anaesthesia was his chosen profession and he enjoyed forty years of a distinguished medical career which included teaching and research.

After retiring from the hospital, he pursued his love of storytelling and the study of paleoanthropology. His first book *Once Upon a Time, Long, Long Ago* was enthusiastically acclaimed by young readers. It was a Silver Birch nominee.

Henry lives in East York with his wife, Ruth. They are the proud parents of three daughters and the happy grandparents of four grandchildren. Now in his eighties, he is planning his third book about Eevo and Sim.

Notes